Forget Me Knot

Crawley Creek Ranch 1

By: Lori King

Edited by: Ekatarina Sayanova
Red Quill Editing
Artwork by: Jess Buffett
Jess Buffett Graphic Designs
Published by: Lori King Books

Blurb

Lacy Denvers has lost her job and lost her way. All she wants to do now is get her career back on track and find some stability again, but first, she wants to mark something off her bucket list: She wants to learn to ride a horse.

Her dream vacation to the Crawley Creek Cattle Ranch turns into a lesson in patience when the North Dakota winter proves unpredictable as ever. Wrapped in a cocoon of snow, Lacy finds the ranch to be a hidden treasure trove of cowboy eye candy, and her mouth is watering even as her brain is telling her to run.

After a devastating tragedy, a young Drannon Russo ended up fostering with the Crawley family, and found a home. He's only moved away once and had to lean on family for support when his dreams were shattered. Being a cowboy on a ranch is a pretty lonely existence. When a beautiful redhead shows up looking for a fresh start he's determined to give them both what they want.

Will this vacation into the heart of cattle country turn out to be a mistake, or will Lacy and Drannon find their future in each other?

Warning: Explicit romance

Dedication

Drannon Ray Gordon, who gave his life for his country in Vietnam.
Thank you for your service.
~Lori

Chapter 1

"You can't keep doing this to yourself, Romeo." Drannon stared down at the half-naked form of his brother sprawled out on the front porch. It was lucky Roman had made so much noise stumbling around drunk, or he might have frozen to death before morning. As it was, he'd woken Drannon from a sound sleep, and as usual, Drannon had gone to his brother's rescue. Dragging Roman's limp body up over his shoulder, and carrying him out of the February night air, he grumbled under his breath, "Going to end up poisoning your blood with alcohol, or get some sort of damn STD. Why the hell do you think you have to bang every woman this side of the Mississippi anyway? Stupid. Just plain ol'stupid is what that is."

There was no response from the unconscious man, but Drannon felt better as he spewed out his feelings on the recurrent situation. For months he and the other guys had been bailing Roman out and cleaning him up after his binge partying sessions. Maybe it was time to give the kid an ultimatum. Dry out and straighten up, or…

It was the "or" that was the problem. Drannon would never be able to kick his brother off the ranch, no matter how stupid he behaved. Crawley Creek was all Roman had, all any of them had, and it belonged to the whole lot of them.

With one final curse, he dumped Roman onto the sofa and headed for the kitchen in search of a midnight snack. The bright light of the fridge made him squint as he reached for the milk to go with the cookies he knew Marilyn had just put in the cookie jar.

"I thought I heard something." Vin's voice startled him, and he choked on his cookie spewing crumbs all over the counter top. Laughing, Vin slapped him on the back, "Sorry D, didn't mean to scare you. Didn't you bring your teddy-bear downstairs with you?"

"Asshole," Drannon grumbled, reaching for a napkin to wipe his face. "The teddy bear is passed out on the sofa, probably drooling all over Marilyn's fancy pillows, and mumbling to himself, as usual."

Vin's eyes narrowed, and he shook his head. "Not again."

"Yep. Found him on the porch minus his coat, shirt and boots."

"Fuck. That kid is trying to kill himself." Vin took a seat at the breakfast bar, and swiped a cookie from the jar. "Who'd he go out with tonight?"

"No clue, but he smells like cheap perfume and cigarettes. I was half tempted to dunk him in the horse tank before I brought him in, but that isn't fair to the horses." Drannon snorted at his own joke. Roman Freemont, aka Romeo, was only ten years younger than he and Vin, but he acted like a teenager. Partying, and womanizing like it was going out of style. "We're going to have to do something about it."

"Yeah, but I don't have a clue what." Vin scraped his nails over his shaved head in a gesture that was as routine as breathing for him. "He's been tore up ever since…"

His words drifted off, but Drannon nodded his understanding. Less than a year ago, Abraham Crawley had died of a sudden heart attack while fixing a fence in the west pasture. Roman was supposed to have gone with him that day to help him make the repairs, but he'd spent the night at a lady friend's house, and hadn't gotten home in time, so Abe had left on his own. Roman held on to the crazy idea that if he'd been there with Abe he could have saved him, even though the doctors insisted Abe had died almost instantly.

"Guilt's still eating him alive inside." Drannon said, sighing heavily as the sweets he'd consumed turned into a heavy lump in his belly. "He needs help."

"Yep, but he's too stubborn to admit it."

"Just like someone else I know," Drannon shot back with a pointed look at Vin.

His brother's nostrils flared, and his eyes darkened in the murky kitchen lighting. "What's that supposed to mean?"

"Like you don't know? You go all Incredible Hulk on everyone at the slightest thing lately. That PTSD isn't something to play around with, Vin. You need to get back on those meds." Drannon hated pointing it out, especially this late at night, but the opportunity had presented itself, and he couldn't let it go.

"That medicine makes me numb. I'd rather feel something than nothing," Vin grumbled. "Besides, it ain't my fault the guys you hired last summer are morons. Shit, if we had some hands with brains around here maybe I wouldn't lose my temper so much."

It was an argument Vin had made for too long, but Drannon let it drop because two a.m. was not the time to get into it with his brother.

"I'm going back to bed. We have an empty house until Thursday, but then we get a guest." Drannon put the milk away, and wiped the crumbs from the counter into his palm.

Vin frowned back at him as he put the cookie jar away, "A guest? In February?"

"I know, but they booked it a while ago, and it's already paid for. I can't imagine anyone taking a trip to the Dakotas in the dead of winter for fun, but whatever. Money is money, and if we're going to start taking in fosters this summer, we need what we can get."

Following Drannon into the main hallway, Vin nodded, "True that. Want me to take him upstairs?" He gestured toward the living room where Roman's snores rumbled.

Drannon shook his head, "Don't bother. Marilyn will lay into him when she finds him in the morning, and he deserves what he gets."

"That's stone cold, man," Vin said with a chuckle, "but I like it."

The two parted ways, with Drannon heading up the main staircase to the original wing of the house, and Vin heading farther down the hallway to the new wing that was added a couple of decades ago. Abraham and Seraphina Crawley had turned Crawley Creek Ranch into a home for foster children, and as their small clan of orphans and runaways grew, they kept adding on to the main house until it was obvious they needed more space. Cabins sprang up all over the back forty acres, and after the kids grew up and moved away, the buildings stood empty.

Walking through the silence in the dimly lit hallway regularly brought back the memory of how Drannon came to be at Crawley Creek, and he let himself drift back thirty years on a memory.

No one ever told Drannon outright that his mother was dead, but it wasn't hard to figure out. All around him, people avoided his questioning gaze until he stopped looking altogether. The doctor gave him an uncomfortable one-armed hug, and told him that everything would be okay, but the stately man left unspoken the phrase that would shatter a child's eight-year-old heart.

It didn't matter that Elena Russo was a drug addict who frequently sold her body to men in order to buy peanut butter and bread to keep in the cupboards of their tiny one bedroom apartment. All that mattered was that she was his mom and the only person in the world who had ever loved him. Now she was gone. A victim of her own demons.

After several hours of lonely boredom in the tiny hospital waiting room, a tired looking woman with dark coffee-colored skin, her hair pulled back in a severe bun, arrived to collect him. By the time she'd completed the hospital's necessary release paperwork, Drannon was near to falling over with hunger and exhaustion.

"Hello Drannon, my name is Danica. I'm with social services, and I'm going to get you someplace more comfortable so that you can get some rest. It's been a trying day for you hasn't it, sugar?" Her voice was raspy but comforting after the haunted silence of the last hours alone wondering and worrying. When she cocked her head and frowned, he nodded quickly, feeling his cheeks heat. "Do you have anything with you?"

He shook his head no, thinking briefly of the three t-shirts and two pairs of torn jeans resting in the bottom drawer of his mother's dresser. It wasn't much, but it was all he had. Clearing his throat he tried to tell her. "M-my c-clothes, um…they're in m-my house…er…ap-ap-apartment."

Embarrassment filled him making the stuttering even worse as he struggled to get the words out. Danica nodded, but her eyes were sad. "Unfortunately, the police have the apartment roped off while they do their investigation, but I'll do my best to collect whatever you need from there tomorrow. For tonight, we'll just have to make do."

She didn't mention the stuttering at all, and his anxiety eased. When she reached for his hand, he gratefully accepted the gesture. There was no way she could know that it was the first time in his life he could remember anyone holding his hand. Following her lead, they left the hospital that held the empty body that was his mother, and went directly from there to a fast food restaurant where Danica let him choose anything he wanted off the menu.

After a large cheeseburger and fries washed down by an enormous cola, his eyelids began to droop heavily. He didn't remember anything about the ride other than climbing into the car and buckling his seat belt. On that frigid February night, all that mattered was that he was full for the first time in months, and comfortably tucked in front of the heat vent in Danica's car.

She woke him when they parked in front of a massive white ranch house that had a wrap-around front porch. Drannon couldn't see much more in the dark, but he got the impression of other buildings off to his left as he followed Danica to the front door. A tall man with dark hair and a mustache that looked like a huge caterpillar swung it open and gestured them inside.

"Who have we here?" the man's voice was deep, and it brought a shiver to Drannon's spine as it reverberated in the foyer and on down the wide hallway.

"This is Drannon." Danica answered, patting his shoulder hard enough that he had to take another step further into the house. "Drannon, this is Abraham Crawley. He owns the ranch, and he and his wife will be your guardians until we find you a permanent place to stay."

"Drannon?" Abraham's eyebrow rose. "Strong name. Do you have a last name, son?"

His throat was drier than the desert, but he managed to force out a reply. "R-Ru-Russo."

"Drannon Russo, yes sir, that's a strong name. Italian last name, I believe. Tell me son, do you have a strong backbone to match that name?" Abraham looked him over as if he was measuring up a man his own size, and Drannon felt his chest puff out in an attempt to live up to the other man's estimation of him.

"Y-yes s-sir." He said, grimacing at the repetitive sounds. Over the last couple of years he'd managed to get a handle on his stuttering, but the moment he found his mother sprawled out on the bathroom floor with her face covered in her own vomit, he lost all control over his own tongue.

Like Danica, Abraham didn't react to the stuttering, and Drannon breathed a sigh of relief. It was hard enough to speak to adults, much less disappoint them when they heard him slip up. He realized Danica was talking to Abraham and tuned back in to the conversation. "...release the body from the coroner's office tomorrow. So far we haven't located any living relatives."

A soft voice tinkled from behind where Abraham's broad shoulders blocked the opening from the foyer into the rest of the house, "So sad. I'm sure she was way too young. Well, anyways, it's lovely to meet you, Drannon, no matter the circumstances."

For the first time, Drannon noticed a petite woman with braided brunette hair standing just behind Abraham. The way she slid under his arm against his side, assured Drannon that she was the lady of the house, and he nodded his thanks to her without speaking.

"*Drannon, I'd like you to meet my wife, Seraphina Crawley.*" *Abraham looked down at the smiling woman with pride. For just a moment, Drannon felt envious of Seraphina. What would it be like to have such a strong man look at him with pride? He couldn't remember his mother looking at him with anything but affection and obligation. Although he knew she loved him, he'd always come second to her addiction.*

"*Call me Sera; only Abe gets away with using my whole name.*" *Sera's eyes were dark chocolate brown, and her kind smile radiated warmth. Drannon's heart flip-flopped and he fell half in love with her in that moment. "Have you eaten yet?*"

"*We stopped and ate a burger on our way out here. Unfortunately he's been stuck at the hospital most of the day. I was in court or I'd have picked him up earlier. I didn't get the message about his m—er…situation, until after seven.*" *Danica gave him a smile he figured was supposed to be apologetic, but really held only pity. He hated pity. Thankfully there was no pity in the sympathetic gazes Sera and Abe turned on him.*

"*Poor thing. I'm glad you've got a full belly. That will make it a little bit easier to rest tonight. Come on upstairs and I'll show you where you'll be sleeping. We only have one other boy here right now, and he's in the room across from yours. You're lucky it's a quiet time. We've had up to fourteen children here at one time.*" *Without a backwards glance at Danica, Drannon followed the chattering Sera farther into the house and up a wide staircase that split the living room in two. It was an enormous house from the looks of it, but it felt warm and cozy in spite of its size.*

At the top of the stairs she turned and led him to a set of closed doors. Opening the one on the left, she stepped aside for Drannon to enter first. The bedroom was larger than the apartment he'd been living in with his mother, and the bedding covering the massive wood framed bed looked clean and fresh. A thick blue comforter covered the mattress, and a chest of drawers taller than he was, was tucked into the corner. Heavy-looking blue curtains hung over a window opposite the bed, and the whole room smelled like cedar.

"*This is going to be your room; we call it the blue room for obvious reasons. The other young man we have staying with us, Vinnie, is across the hall, you'll meet him at breakfast in the morning. He's been here a while now, so he can show you the ropes. Abe and I are through those double doors at the end of this hall, and there's a bathroom right here,*" *Sera gestured just down the hallway, "You and Vinnie will have to share it, and I don't tolerate fighting, so make sure you get along. You're welcome to use anything you find in the medicine cabinet and linen cupboard, but if you need anything else, you just holler.*"

Drannon's head was spinning. He'd gone from a crack house to a mansion in a day, and somehow, even though he'd lost everything, he couldn't feel the sadness anymore. He wanted to feel sad about his mom. He was going to miss her, but he wasn't going to miss cold nights on the dirty floor while she was tucked away with someone in the only bedroom. And he wasn't going to miss racing to school in the mornings so that he could arrive in time for breakfast because it was the only food he was going to get before class.

Turning back to Sera, he surprised himself when genuine emotion boiled up and his eyes stung, "T-thank y-you, Miss Sera."

"You're welcome, Drannon. This is your home for as long as you need it, and we're glad to have you here. Now, make yourself comfortable. I'll grab you some clothes to sleep in, and if you'll leave your dirty clothes in the laundry hamper tonight, Marilyn will make sure they get washed for you." She bustled into the bathroom, and Drannon followed just far enough to keep his eyes locked on her. He had no idea who Marilyn was, but he didn't really care either. All that he wanted now was to crawl into that big bed, and sleep until he could put this whole nightmarish day behind him.

Sera pulled a brand new toothbrush and toothpaste out of the cabinet behind the mirror in the bathroom, and laid them on the counter. Next came a bar of soap, a washcloth, and a towel. "Do you need help taking a bath, Drannon?" she asked, with a look of concern on her face. He didn't like it when she frowned like that. It made her forehead wrinkle, and she was much prettier smiling.

"N-no ma'am. I c-c-can do it."

Her smile of approval nearly blinded him, "Good. I figured at eight years old you were probably well on your way to taking care of yourself, but like I told you, if you need anything at all, Drannon, just come find me. Okay?"

They watched each other, she with rapt curiosity on her face, and he with wary reservation and admiration for the tiny woman in front of him. He wondered why she was being so nice to him. They were strangers, but she was treating him like family. When her face fell into a sad frown he realized he'd voiced his thoughts, and he immediately took a hesitant step backwards when her hands reached to embrace him.

"You poor dear. I'm so sorry for what you've been through today. No one should have to go through that." Her genuine concern stole his breath and cracked the shield he'd been holding over his emotions all day long. Tears filled his eyes, and his lungs burned as he panted for air. "It's okay, let it out. Cry all you need to. There's no shame in crying when the tears are for someone you love."

The validation meant everything to him, but he couldn't find it in him to respond verbally so he just nodded mutely, and wept against her shoulder. All of the fear and sorrow from the day seemed to leak out of him rolling down his cheeks and soaking into her blouse. When his sobs finally subsided and he was left hiccupping and wiping his snotty nose on his hand, she finally released him.

"There now. You've got that all out of your system, and now you'll sleep better." Tenderly pushing his shaggy hair from his eyes, she brushed her lips across his forehead. "We'll talk when you're ready, but tonight you need to rest. Sleep well, Drannon."

Silently, he watched as she headed off down the hall, turning at the top of the stairs and disappearing from sight. He stood dumbly for several minutes in the doorway of the blue room, taking in his temporary home with a hint of envy for the people who lived here permanently. He assumed by the way Danica spoke it was unlikely he'd be here long, but he was going to take advantage of the luxury while he could. After all, it wasn't like his mother was going to come back to life and scold him for indulging in a bath with real soap.

If he was going to be on his own for the rest of his life, he was going to take advantage of every possible good thing that came along and relish in it while he could. Who knew what kind of home permanent Danica would find for him? For this brief moment, he was safe, surrounded by warmth and people who genuinely cared about his feelings, and that was all he'd ever wanted.

A door opened and closed downstairs, startling Drannon from his reminiscing, and he shook off the lump of emotion in his throat. Abe and Sera became his salvation as he grew into a temperamental young man with an ax to grind. They'd just as easily been his cheerleaders when he finally realized no one owed him anything and he'd have to go out and work for his future. He invested his energies in a career that turned sour on him, and eight years ago, he came home from the big city with his tail between his legs, and found his heart back home on the ranch.

He and his three closest foster brothers, Roman, Vin, and Hawke had bought the ranch off Abe and turned the main house and most of the cabins into a guest ranch. Of course it was Marilyn who ran the guest side of things, while the boys took care of the ranch. It turned out to be a great investment, and a timely one considering Sera died a couple of years later, and the fire inside Abe fizzled.

Now that both Crawleys were gone, the big house seemed cold and empty most days, even when it was full of guests or ranch hands. Skimming his hand up the wide oak banister, Drannon remembered sliding down it on his rump and getting scolded over and over by Sera, who always did it with a smile on her face. He remembered garland wrapped around it with twinkling lights encircling the posts, and the smell of pies and Christmas cookies. This Christmas Marilyn had put up the tree alone, and the tree skirt had remained empty since the boys decided not to bother exchanging gifts with each other. Maybe it wasn't just Abe who lost his heart when

Sera died. The whole of Crawley Creek Ranch seemed to have lost its sparkle.

Pushing aside his sad thoughts, and longing for the old days, Drannon went back to bed already listing in his head the multitude of chores that needed to be done when the sun rose.

Chapter 2

There was absolutely nothing good about Valentine's Day in Lacy's book. It was a waste of money and time. She couldn't understand why people would want to buy chocolates and roses for each other to represent their deepest love. In her mind that gift was like saying, I will love you for a little while and I am going to make you fat before we break up in a few weeks. It was ridiculous.

Her hatred of the holiday might have had something to do with the fact that she had to share it with another special day, her birthday. Yep, she was a sweetheart baby. That meant everyone "ooed" and "awed" when they spotted her birthday on her driver's license, and she had to pretend like it was some great thing. In truth, Lacy had never even had a boyfriend over the holiday, so she'd never had the chance to figure out the attraction to the silliness. For years, each Valentine's day she had been heartbroken to realize that she was alone while everyone else she knew had someone. She'd allowed the desire to have a 'someone' of her own overwhelm her and drag her down.

But this year was different. For her birthday, she was doing something for herself. Something she'd always wanted to do and her father had ridiculed. There would be no sulking because she was alone. She wouldn't be alone. She would be surrounded by horses on a real ranch in North Dakota. She had booked the trip months ago, before she lost her job and started building her own graphic design and marketing company.

It was ironic that she was able to travel wherever she wanted to for a vacation now that she was in the age range when most people settled down.

All of her friends from high school and college were married with children. Some were even divorced once or twice. When most of them were traveling and finding themselves, she was focusing on growing her career. Her twenties were spent in a tiny shoebox apartment in Chicago learning the industry by working for a prestigious marketing firm. But layoffs and downsizing had eliminated her position at the end of the year, and she was forced to figure out a different path.

Today, she was stepping out of her comfort zone with a trip out of the big city and into the deep northern plains. Her taxi pulled up in front of a massive ranch house, and the driver gave her a quick smile in the rearview mirror as he called out, "We're here," and climbed from the car.

With her laptop bag slung over her shoulder, she accepted her suitcase from him and looked over the large ranch where she would be staying. Crawley Creek was a working ranch with more than five thousand head of cattle on it at any given time. According to the kind woman she spoke with when making her reservations, it boasted seven guest rooms in the main house and a handful of guest cabins.

Lacy was hoping the respite from the smog and noise of the city would give her time to decide where she wanted to go with her business and life. Chicago's higher cost of living meant she was barely able to afford to feed herself and keep her business afloat. She was rapidly coming to the conclusion that moving was necessary to her survival when an opportunity appeared in the form of a dog food company. The gig could make her a success, or drain her of her time so she couldn't work on making any other connections in the industry because she was too busy with her one and only client. Not that she would turn the job down if they offered, but she'd been seriously considering if it was the right direction ever since she clicked the submit button on her bid.

Brushing her long red braid over the shoulder of her heavy coat, she forced thoughts of business out of her mind as she headed for the front door while trying to absorb every detail around her. The house looked like it was cut right out of a magazine, with white clapboard siding, and dark green shutters lining each window. A wide porch ran all the way across the front, and around one side, and there was a porch swing and several rocking chairs. Between a pair of them sat a small table with an empty chessboard on it. She could just imagine how serene it would be to play chess there during the warmer months. Snow dusted all the seats, and Lacy

18

grimaced as she considered learning how to ride a horse in the biting cold wind. North Dakota was probably not the ideal vacation spot for most people, but for Lacy it sounded just about perfect. In a couple days, she would be celebrating her birthday as never before—alone in the middle of nowhere, surrounded by nature, silence, and snow, and completely at peace—she hoped.

The front door opened wide as she climbed the steps, and a shorter, round woman with shoulder length platinum blonde hair stepped out to greet her. A towel was thrown over her wide shoulder, and there was a streak of white powder across her ample breasts. She smiled at Lacy as she shivered in the cold. "Miss Denvers, I presume?"

"Yes. Lacy, please."

"Come on in Lacy, and make yourself comfortable. It's far too cold to be standing on the porch at this time of year. I'm Marilyn Monroe, the housekeeper and cook for Crawley Creek."

Lacy felt her mouth curve up in a grin at the woman's introduction, and Marilyn caught it. "No relation to the starlet, although I know how much we look alike." She gave Lacy a wicked grin and the two women shared a laugh. Marilyn was only about five foot five and her face was deeply etched with laugh lines and crow's feet. Her blue eyes were warm and friendly, and Lacy liked her immediately.

"Well, now, I can tell the whole world that I've met Marilyn Monroe."

Marilyn waved her off as she took her coat, "You can tell them my dear, but I don't expect it will change too much. I have yet to give out any autographs living up here. Now, I've put you in the lilac room here in the main house. We don't have any other guests right now, and with another snow scheduled in just a couple of days I didn't want you to have to trudge in and out of the cold more than was necessary. I hope that's all right."

"Sure, thank you."

Lacy finished removing her tennis shoes and tucked them under the bench by the door before following Marilyn down the hallway into the main living room. It was two stories tall, but unusually cozy, and she couldn't resist running her hand over the glossy black finish on a baby grand piano that sat next to a massive staircase. The way the stairs curved reminded her of Scarlett O'Hara in *Gone with the Wind,* and she felt important climbing them. At the top, Marilyn turned right, and led her down the hallway to a closed door.

"Here we are, my dear. You'll find the bathroom is through that door across the hall, and you'll have free reign of the house while you're here. I live downstairs in a small apartment behind the kitchen, and the only other soul in this wing of the house right now is Drannon. His room is at the other end of the hallway. The other fellas live in the back wing, or in the bunk house. Besides the owners, we have about two dozen ranch hands that you'll see around the property during the day, but they will all be wearing a Crawley Creek coat as cold as it is, so you'll know they work here."

Lacy looked where Marilyn was pointing and counted at least four doors down the other side of the upstairs hallway. It ended in a massive pair of carved wooden doors that exemplified elegant importance. Obviously, the infamous owner, Drannon, lived behind that statement piece, she thought wryly. Guessing which door was the owner's personal bedroom was the least of her concerns right now, so instead she turned back and stepped into the Lilac room.

It was clear how the room got its name. There was a soft lilac-colored quilt on the enormous brass bed that dominated the room. Matching curtains hung on a pair of windows that faced east, and Lacy smiled as she imagined waking up with the sunrise streaming through them in the morning. Cream-colored wallpaper covered the walls, and a pair of sage green reading chairs sat to one side with a small table between them. An enormous antique chest of drawers sat on the other side of the bed, with an antique lamp on top. The room was beautiful and tastefully done. Lacy loved it immediately.

"I will have dinner ready about six thirty, um, we usually just serve dinner in the dining room as a group event, but if you'd rather eat alone..."

Lacy shook her head, "No, I'll join you guys."

"Wonderful! Tonight, I put a pot roast on. I hope you aren't one of those non-meat eaters?"

"No ma'am. I'm not a vegetarian. I like a good steak, and a pot roast sounds perfect to me. The room is lovely," She turned back to the bed and dropped her luggage next to it, while laying her laptop bag down a little more carefully. "You said the bathroom is across the hallway?"

"Oh yes, the door right there directly across from you. These old houses weren't built with bathrooms for each bedroom, so periodically, we have to ask guests to share if the cabins are full up, but with no other guests, you'll have it to yourself. If you'd prefer a cabin we can certainly get one readied for you, but..."

Lacy immediately shook her head, "No, thank you. Like I said, this will be just perfect."

"Wonderful. Feel free to explore the house. There is a study downstairs with a small library of sorts; you're welcome to set up your computer there, but mind you, the internet can be spotty way out here under the best of circumstances. When you're ready I can have one of the guys give you the nickel tour of the barns. How does that sound?"

Marilyn looked so bright and excited that Lacy had to return her smile. "It all sounds great. Thank you, Marilyn. I think I'll take a walk around and look things over myself for now. I don't want to be a bother to anyone. I'm here to learn how to sit in a saddle, rest and make decisions about the rest of my life in peace and quiet."

Marilyn snorted a little laugh, "Well peace and quiet we certainly have in abundance in the winter time here. In fact, some winters we've been snowed in for weeks at a time with only each other for entertainment. It can make a girl stir crazy real quick being surrounded by testosterone and cattle. Breakfast is at six in the dining room, or if you want to sleep late holler at me, and I can bring a tray up later. We're happy to have you here at Crawley Creek. If there is anything at all I can do to make your stay more enjoyable, just let me know."

Marilyn bustled out of the bedroom and back downstairs leaving Lacy to her own devices. The smile on her face didn't dim as she ran her hand over the bed and then across the glowing oak of the end table beside it. The room reminded her of something she might see in an old western movie, and her brain was spinning with excitement. Leaving her suitcase packed, she went across the hallway to check out the bathroom.

She was pleased to find a modern walk-in steam shower as well as a wide soaking tub, and a separate lavatory. She was glad she wouldn't be sharing it with anyone, and she made a mental note to sink into a hot tub of bubbles later in the evening. A good book with a glass of wine and a soak in the tub seemed like the perfect way to spend her first night on vacation.

Making her way down her wing of the hallway, she took the liberty of peeking in the other guest rooms since there were no other guests. Each room was beautifully decorated with a blend of modern and antique furnishings, and each was clearly labelled on the door with a theme. The one next to hers was the sunflower room, and it was decorated just as cheerfully as its name suggested. Across the hallway, were the President's room, and the Captain's room. Both were decorated with a more masculine touch, but they were all simple and classy.

She decided that she liked the air of mystery that surrounded the other hallway, so she didn't bother exploring it any further and made her way back downstairs. Wandering all over the ranch house she found the same eclectic mix of heirloom-quality tables and dressers, and updated modern conveniences like a closet with a stackable washer and dryer, and a large gathering room with comfy looking sofas and a flat screen TV. It wasn't until she hit the study that she truly felt transported into another era.

The room was paneled in dark wood, and an enormous desk filled most of the floor space on one end, and a stone fireplace dominated the other end. A heavy duty leather desk chair sat behind the desk, and an antique blotter and gas lamp were the only items on top. An elegant ladies chaise lounge sat opposite a pair of masculine leather wingback chairs, and two of the four walls were covered ceiling to floor in bookshelves that were bursting with books.

She found everything from *Dante's Inferno* and *Little Women*, to the more risqué *Sleeping Beauty Trilogy* by A. N. Roquelaure. It was as though the owners were as eclectic in their reading tastes as they were in their decorating. Browsing the selections she found herself more and more intrigued by the rancher who loved to read. It certainly shattered all of the preconceived notions she had about cowboys.

Although she was tempted to settle into one of the chairs and lose herself in a good book, there was still a little daylight out, and she had a whole ranch to explore. She retrieved her coat from the hook by the door and bundled up with her hood tucked tightly around her head. Her red braid hung in front of her because it was too awkward to force it into the coat, and she shoved her feet back into her shoes before stepping outside.

The wind was still blowing, and it had taken on a sharper, frostier feel, quickly biting through the denim of her jeans. If it stayed this cold, it was unlikely that Lacy would spend much time riding horses this week, but she was still determined to meet a few.

There was a couple of inches of snowdrift across the front lawn, but when she turned the corner and faced west, brown grass poked through a dusting of snow, and the wind stole her breath from her lungs. Grey clouds filled the sky and the scent of snow was on the air. Tipping her head down, she hurried across the yard to the massive barn doors, pausing only long enough to tug one open and squeeze through it.

Compared to the cold outside, the warmth of the barn was intoxicating. The smell of animals and hay filled her nose, and she sneezed loudly.

"Bless you."

The deep voice was followed by a masculine chuckle, and she jerked in surprise looking for its owner. When she didn't immediately spot anyone, she frowned.

"Thank you, um, whoever you are?"

A black cowboy hat appeared over the top of a stall next to a brown horse's head. Under the hat was a strong face with a sharp jaw and a meticulously trimmed goatee and mustache. His nose was a little large, and as she stepped closer she could see that it was also slightly crooked with a telling bump in the middle. The smile on his face was amused as he allowed her to look her fill. But he raised one black eyebrow when she remained standing quietly several feet away from him.

Concern filled his brown eyes, and he reached one long arm over the stall door opening the latch. Her vision suddenly filled with the huge, sexy body of a real life cowboy and she felt her chest tighten. He was beautiful. Black, curly hair peeked out from under the brim of his hat, barely curling over his ears and the collar of his heavy brown coat. His wide shoulders filled out every spare millimeter of the material, and a powerfully built chest drew her gaze further down until her eyes struck gold. Framed by perfectly cut chaps was a thick looking bulge of blue denim and zipper, and Lacy nearly groaned out loud at the many wicked images running through her brain.

"Are you all right?"

She jumped in surprise at his question and felt a hot blush creep up her cheeks. "Yes, I'm sorry. That was ridiculously rude, please excuse me." She stepped forward with her hand out, "I'm Lacy Denvers."

"Ah, yes Marilyn said we were going to have a guest for a couple of weeks." The hand that took hers was enormous, and it engulfed her grip until she could barely see her own skin. She could feel calluses on his palm, and a shiver went up her spine at the raspy touch. What would that feel like on other more sensitive parts of her body? "Pretty unusual for someone to book a vacation in North Dakota in the winter."

She was taken aback by the comment and frowned up at him. At five foot eight, Lacy wasn't a short girl, but the cowboy was at least four or five inches taller than she was, so she had to tip her head back to see his eyes. "I booked the trip last summer. I wanted to get away from the city, and I wanted to learn how to ride. Is that a problem?"

"Want to learn how to ride, huh?" The teasing flirtation in his voice made her pussy clench and her breasts swell. This time it was *his* eyes that slowly wandered down her body taking in every bit of her before coming back up to meet her pointed gaze. "I have no doubt that you can learn how to ride like a pro here at Crawley Creek."

She nodded sharply refusing to acknowledge the innuendo. His eyes had turned a darker color, and his pupils had grown along with the bulge behind his zipper. The attraction was clearly mutual. Her heart was racing in her chest, and she turned back to the horse he had been working with in order to give herself some breathing room.

"She's pretty; does she have a name?"

The cowboy stepped closer to the stall. Her palms were suddenly sweating, too. She was glad she had on so many layers so that he wouldn't be able to see the hard nubs of her nipples poking through her shirt.

"She is a he, and his name is Toto." Lacy snorted and then covered her mouth in embarrassment. "Sorry, you don't mean Toto like the dog in Oz do you?"

"Is there another Toto?"

A giggle slipped out, and then turned into a full on loud laugh. Toto snuffed in his stall and looked at her with large brown eyes. The cowboy seemed amused at her enjoyment. He stepped closer and reached his hand up to run it over Toto's forehead. The horse nuzzled him, and bobbed its head asking for more affection.

"Here, reach up and touch him. He's like any other male, if you stroke him right he'll be yours forever." His voice was low and deep, and his eyes were locked on Lacy while she reached up to run her hand over the soft white spot on Toto's forehead. Toto truly did seem to appreciate the gesture, and he tipped his nose to sniff at her arm.

"He's beautiful. This is the closest I've ever been to a real horse."

"Toto is honored to be your first."

Lacy's eyes darted over to look at the cowboy. His flirtations weren't subtle, and his eyes blatantly said that he would be up for a hot, sweaty fling. She pondered for less than a breath before she turned to face him.

"Are all of the Crawley Creek cowboys this forward?" She cocked her head to one side watching him. His eyes shuttered and the heat seemed to seep out of them instantly.

"I apologize. It's not often a beautiful woman appears in the barn out of nowhere. I have some more work to do, but you're welcome to look around, just make sure to stay out of the stalls without someone with you. All of the horses are gentle most of the time, but accidents happen. You're such a wisp, one kick and you'd be done for." While he spoke, he reached back over the wall of the stall and pulled up a bucket that must have been on a hook inside. There was a collection of unusual tools inside the bucket, but she didn't have a chance to ask him what they were before he was headed down the walkway and out the doors.

Chapter 3

Drannon cursed himself for not thinking before he spoke. Humiliation burned in his belly as he marched out of the barn with his spine stiff. This wasn't Chicago, this was Montford, North Dakota, and women didn't like to be flirted with in such an obvious way. Maybe some of the ones Roman hung out with did, but he didn't even know this Lacy woman, and he'd very nearly pushed her up against the barn stall and kissed her breathless. Good lord, he was losing his mind. He hadn't even bothered to make sure she was single before he hit on her.

Dropping his tool bucket on the concrete floor of the garage that held both vehicles and farm equipment, he tugged off his hat, and ran his fingers through his hair as he looked for Vin. A pair of coverall clad legs poked out from under a seventy-six Ford pickup truck that had seen better days, and Drannon headed that way.

"Hey Vin, did you ever hear from Laslo about the spreader he wanted to sell?" Drannon rested his backside against the fender of a Bronco that Hawke had driven years before until it nearly fell to pieces on him.

From under the truck, Vin's voice sounded garbled, "Nope, but I can call him later. I've almost got this one done, and then I have to figure out what happened with the Johnny tractor before I can call it quits for today."

"Snow's coming in. I can smell it." Drannon said, letting his eyes drift closed as he thought about the pretty redheaded guest in the barn. A secret part of him was hoping there would be a lot of snow so he'd be stuck inside with Lacy.

"Yeah, every nimwit in the county is probably in town at the grocery store right now. Did you check with Marilyn to see if she needs anything?" Vin called out.

"I just finished changing Toto's shoes, but I was headed inside shortly. We have a guest, so I'm sure she planned ahead."

Vin rolled out from under the truck, and sat up, wiping his hands on his pant legs. Before he could say anything, Hawke's blonde head appeared in the door way. A cold gust of wind followed him inside lifting his long locks and skewing them over his eyes.

"Shit it's colder than a witch's tit," Hawke grumbled as he rubbed his hands together and headed towards the two of them. "What's this pow wow about?"

"Just bullshitting." Drannon answered. "Did you get the stragglers?"

Hawke had been out all morning searching for several of their cattle that had gone missing when they herded them back to the interior pasture ahead of the storm. He nodded. "Yep, Daisy was down in the ditch as always, and the others got caught up on the wrong side of Soffet's pond. We've got'em all now."

"Good, we can't afford to lose many this winter," Drannon said firmly. The ranch made a good income, but the plan that the four of them had for the future was going to take more, so it was important that they kept a close eye on losses this year. "Heads up. Our guest is here, so be on your best behavior tonight."

Hawke grimaced, "Damn, I was hoping to play Xbox on the big screen for the next week while we waited out the storm."

Drannon grinned and shook his head. "You and that damn game system. I'm sure Miss Denvers won't give a damn if you're in the family room gaming while she's here."

"Miss? We have a female guest?" Hawke's blue eyes lit up.

A strange thing happened inside Drannon's chest at the obvious interest from his brother, and he had to bite back a snarl. "Yes, she's female, but that doesn't mean she's available. Just mind your manners."

Hawke snapped a mock salute, and tapped the heels of his cowboy boots together, "Aye aye Cap'n."

Vin was laughing as Drannon headed out of the garage and toward the main house to clean up before dinner. Clearly, finding a minute alone with Lacy to apologize was necessary because his brothers were going to be all over her the moment they laid eyes on the fiery beauty. He just had to get there first.

~ ~ ~ ~

Lacy stood in the barn for a few moments staring after the hot cowboy in shock. She hadn't intended on scaring him away. In fact, she had been ready to have a quick roll in the hay with him just to see if he could bring the heat his eyes had promised. Instead, she had offended him somehow and she hadn't even managed to get his name before he disappeared.

Toto pushed against her shoulder with his nose catching her off balance and making her laugh.

"Well, at least I've managed to hold one male's attention today. That's one more than I've had for about five years. You sure are beautiful Toto, even if you are a boy. Maybe I can convince that skittish cowboy to let me ride you tomorrow. What do you think?" She giggled again when Toto let out a huffing sound and moved over to start eating hay.

Her urge to explore was gone. Now, she had wet panties and aching breasts that weren't going to go away on their own. Wrapping her coat tighter around her middle, she hurried back into the ranch house. If she couldn't find a cowboy to scratch her itch, then she would scratch it herself, damn it. With a quick wave to Marilyn after removing her outerwear, she hurried up to her room and locked the door behind her.

The only child of a single dad, Lacy hadn't really had anyone to give her instruction or explanation about her own desires. A few muddled encounters had gotten rid of her virginity while managing to leave her grossly unsatisfied and naïve. She almost pitied the next relationship she entered, because she had a whole lot of making up to do for time lost.

Settling on the bed, she let her mind run back through the conversation in the barn. Her body had certainly reacted to the hot cowboy, but that wasn't a good enough reason to jump him without knowing him. No matter how much the well-built man turned her on, now was not the time to be getting tangled up in a fling. Hell, he'd probably get fired if the owners found out one of their ranch hands was hooking up with a guest. She'd feel terrible if she got someone fired just to ease her own libido.

There was only one thing she could do at this point to satisfy the need he'd built inside of her. Pushing her shirt up, she pinched her nipples through her bra, and teased them until they were aching peaks. Her hand skimmed over her own belly, beneath her jeans to her pussy, and she imagined how her skittish cowboy would react if he could see the state he'd left her in. Would he sit in the chair across the room to watch, or would he join her on the bed, spreading her thighs and sliding his fingers through her wetness.

She could almost feel his hands pulling her jeans off so that he could grip her upper thighs and open her wide. In her fantasy, she could feel the sensation of his fingers rubbing little circles over her clit before dipping into the creamy moisture that was dripping from her passage. He was big all over, and she warmed considerably when she imagined his thick fingers pushing their way into her pussy, filling her and stretching her to prepare her for an equally thick cock.

She rocked her hips, as her fingers found a natural motion on her most delicate parts, bringing her and her fantasies to a quick and satisfying end. A soft moan slipped from her lips as her body shuddered and jerked, sated for the moment. Immediately, she felt ashamed to be fantasizing about a stranger. Perhaps if she had just let him flirt a little longer she would have at least gotten a name out of him.

Irritated with herself, she redressed, and spent the next ten minutes unpacking her bags into the chest of drawers. With her laptop in hand, she headed downstairs to the study. One of those wing back chairs would be the perfect place to settle while she checked her email for news from her potential clients.

If she could secure that contract with the dog food company it would mean redesigning and rebuilding their website, creating and maintaining their marketing plan, and it would ultimately pay big bucks. But it would also mean that she would be tied to Chicago for at least another year while she fulfilled the contract. It would be a huge milestone in her career, but it would mean so much more to her life. So, why was she dreading getting the email so much?

Chapter 4

Drannon went through the back door this time so that he could avoid running into Lacy again before he had a chance to get the smell of animals off his skin. He was praying that he hadn't screwed up too much in their first meeting. He so rarely met a woman who made his balls tingle, that he felt like he couldn't afford to flub it up when he apologized. If she was single, he was damn sure going to make sure she knew he was interested.

A feeling of guilt made his throat tighten, and he frowned at himself in the bathroom mirror as he stripped down. It was a good thing she was only here for two weeks. If they did have a fling, there wouldn't be enough time to royally fuck her life up before she headed back to wherever she was from. He was good at screwing things up.

He'd managed to get Vin arrested and put in prison, fuck up his first career with his own naïveté, and he had a failed marriage under his belt. Hell, what more could he possibly do to prove his ineptitude? It seemed the only thing he was good at was taking care of the ranch and the animals.

Water so hot it scalded his skin, washed over him, and he forced himself away from the poor me attitude he settled into so easily. It was comfortable to blame himself for everything that went wrong in the world, but as Vin's therapist continuously told them, guilt didn't do anyone any good.

Soap bubbles trickled over the black ink on his left rib cage, and he murmured the words to himself. Growth before pride. It had become his mantra, and he had to tell himself continuously that he was growing as a person. Lately, he believed it less and less. His life had become stagnant.

He didn't go off the ranch except for the occasional supply run or night at the bar in town. At the rate he was going, he'd die a lonely, self-pitying man.

The sound of his bedroom door opening drew him from his musings, and he poked his head out of the shower. "Who's in here?"

"It's me, D." Roman's voice sounded hollow through the bathroom door separating them.

"I'll be out in a sec." Drannon called, shutting the water off. His brothers rarely came to his side of the house. They lived in the new wing, and felt like the old wing brought back too many painful memories. It was the opposite for him. He felt Sera and Abe's presence in the master bedroom, and he felt like it boded well for his future that his brothers assigned him that space. Someday, he hoped to settle down with someone and raise a family in the same house where he'd found a home thirty years before.

Wrapping a thick towel around his waist he stepped through into the bedroom. "What's up Romeo?"

"Sorry, I didn't know you were showering. I can come back," Roman started to say. Drannon frowned at the younger man.

"Nah, I'm good, just going to pull on something clean so I don't offend our guest with my stench. What brings you to this side of the house?" Drannon dropped the towel and slid on a pair of boxer briefs as Roman turned to stare out the massive windows that faced the pasture.

"Sorry about last night."

"Which part? The part where you got drunk and drove yourself home, or the part where your drunk ass woke me up and ruined my wet dream?" Drannon teased.

As expected, his joke made Roman chuckle and shake his head. "Both. I didn't plan to get lit last night, but Bran got the news that he was being promoted to Sheriff yesterday."

"He did? Damn! Good for him! So Randy finally retired?"

Brandon Bowers had been Hawke and Roman's third musketeer growing up. They'd attended the same schools, even though Bran had never been a resident of Crawley Creek. He'd gone straight into law enforcement after college, and Drannon had always expected him to move up the ladder and run a big inner city police department, but Bran had settled in with the Montford Sheriff's Department. They continued to be friends, but they'd lost some of the closeness after Drannon and Vin both spent time behind bars.

"Yep, his last day is at the end of the month, and that's when Bran takes over officially." Roman explained.

"Guess you're gonna have to clean your shit up. Bran isn't going to be as easy on you as Randy was." Drannon sat on the bed to pull his socks and boots back on.

Roman snorted a laugh. "Randy was *easy* on me?"

"He never pressed charges for drunk and disorderly, or drunk driving for that matter."

"No, he just took me in and made me sleep in that damn drunk tank. I hate that fucking tiny space. Feels like the walls are closing in." Roman shivered and rubbed at his arms. Drannon knew his brother had a fear of enclosed spaces, but it was Roman's own fault that he kept getting carted into the tiny holding cell.

"Stop drinking and you'll stop having to enjoy the Sheriff's hospitality."

Roman shook his head, "Look I didn't come up here for a lecture. I just wanted to say I'm sorry."

"Yeah, me too. I just wish you really knew what you were sorry about." With that Drannon left his younger brother standing next to the window in his room, and headed downstairs to confront his own issues. Roman had yet to admit that he was fighting addiction, and until he faced his guilt over the past, he'd never win the battle. Unfortunately, there wasn't much Drannon could do to help him. The more he pushed, the harder Roman resisted, and the bigger playboy he became. Only time would tell if Roman's guilt would be his downfall.

~ ~ ~ ~

The door to the study was open, and a fire had been lit in the fireplace. Making herself at home, Lacy had pulled a small round ottoman over so that she could put her socked feet on it while she worked. She had been immersed in the internet for a little while when the heavy thud of boots coming down the hall grabbed her attention. Her eyes lifted and met a pair of familiar dark brown ones.

His curly hair was damp, and he wore a button down shirt tucked into fresh blue jeans. He no longer wore the heavy canvas coat and chaps, but he still looked like a perfect cowboy to her. She had to consciously force herself not to lick her lips as she looked him over. The cowboy gave her a wary glance, pausing in the doorway, before he seemed to find his resolve. His shoulders suddenly seemed broader and his chin jutted out with determination. "Miss Denvers, I owe you an apology—"

Lacy held her hand up to stop him, "No, you don't. I'm tougher than I look. No cowboy is going to ruffle my feathers with a few compliments." She smiled at the relief on his face. "You do owe me something, though."

His thick black eyebrow rose, "Really? What's that?"

"All of that flirting, and you never managed to tell me your name. I think you owe me that after getting me all worked up and walking away."

The cowboy's mouth dropped open just before his nostrils flared and his eyes lit up. "All worked up, huh?" His movements were slow and steady. Like a predator after his prey, he made his way across the room until he stood before her. Her seat on the low slung wingback chair, put her at eye level with that tantalizing bulge under his zipper, and damned if her mouth wasn't watering.

She let out a shaky breath and forced her eyes upwards to meet his. They were a rich brown like worn leather, and she wanted to sink into them and let him have her body completely. Never before had she imagined she would fall weak to a man wearing blue jeans and cowboy boots, but the whole image tripped her trigger making her hotter and wetter than she had ever been before.

"My name is—" he hesitated, before continuing, "Drannon Russo."

Her stomach plummeted and ice shot through her veins. "Oh shit. You're one of the owners."

He gave a short nod, but he kept those penetrating eyes locked on hers. They both waited in silence for the other to speak. Lacy wasn't sure what to say. She was flirting with the ranch owner, not a regular cowboy. This man probably had more money than she had hairs on her head. There was no way she could have a fling with him now.

Shuffling her laptop she shut it down, and stood up. Their bodies were inches away from each other, and she could feel his body heat singeing the skin of her bare arm. The same arm that had given her an explosive orgasm just a few minutes ago, while she fantasized about him.

"I, um, I think I'm done now. I better put this away before dinner." She took a small step sideways, with her laptop under one arm. She started to push her braid back over her shoulder, and he stopped her.

His hand enveloped the end of her thick red braid, holding it and keeping her from moving away. "Don't run off Miss Denvers—"

"Lacy."

Their eyes met and held, bringing a small smile to his full lips. Seductive lips that she could imagine running over her skin, and sucking at her nipples. God, this man was delicious. Why did he have to be the ranch owner?

"I'm sorry I didn't speak up and tell you who I was. Most of the time, I'm introduced to guests at the dinner table, so they already know who I am before I can even speak with them. It's rare that I get a chance to meet a sexy woman—and flirt with her—before she knows how much I'm worth. I enjoyed it immensely."

Lacy couldn't stop the side of her mouth from drawing up in a sardonic smile. "I'm glad I could bring you some measure of pleasure today; however, you and I both know that this can't go any further Mr. Russo."

"Drannon."

She didn't respond, and a low growl rattled from his throat. "My name is Drannon to you, Lacy." She held her ground, with her lips closed, but her heart rate increased when he tugged her by the braid just a few inches closer. She could feel his breath on her cheek, and it smelled like chocolate and mint. "Say my name Lacy, please?"

Her breath caught in her chest, and she inhaled sharply when his lips ran over the skin of her jaw. Goose bumps popped up all over her body and she sighed with pleasure. "Drannon, please…"

That seemed to be the magic word. Suddenly her breasts were pressed against his broad chest, and her braid was wrapped around his fist while his lips savaged hers. He pushed his tongue between her lips and stroked it over her own. She moaned into the kiss and reached up to grip the back of his neck. His curly hair tangled in her fingers, and he gasped when she tugged before he returned the gesture with her braid. Her brain went blank as she turned herself over to the sensation.

Releasing her hair, he gripped her ass in his two massive hands and pulled her even tighter to him, sliding one thick thigh between hers. She couldn't stop herself from grinding against the hard muscle, her already sensitive clit leading the way as she sought satisfaction.

They battled for control, nipping, stroking, and suckling at each other's mouths as if each was starving for the other. Lacy loved the way his big hands held her so easily in his grip refusing to let her move an inch away from where he wanted her. The silent power he wielded made her clench her thighs tighter around his leg as she enjoyed the pressure against her pussy. Higher and higher they both climbed in their desire to touch and taste each other, and just when Lacy had decided to throw caution to the wind and let him fuck her right there on the floor, a voice shattered the veil of passion around them.

Marilyn was standing in the doorway with her back to them, attempting to get their attention while trying to give them privacy.

"I'm so sorry, but dinner is on the table, and I would hate for it to get cold. Would you prefer I put it in the oven until uh…well…um…until you're ready for it?"

Drannon's eyes sparkled with amusement, and he quirked that one damn eyebrow at Lacy again, to let her make the decision. She shook her head slightly, and pulled away from him. Marilyn had just rescued her from making a terrible mistake based on lust and not logic. She was grateful and irritated all at once.

"No need Marilyn, we'll be in shortly. Thank you." Drannon spoke softly, and Lacy grew more irritated at the control he seemed to have over his own emotions. The passionate cowboy who was ready to ravage her a moment ago had disappeared in an instant, leaving behind Mr. Calm Cool & Collected in his place. "May I escort you to dinner, Lacy?"

She frowned at him and glanced to the hallway to be sure Marilyn was gone before speaking. "That was a mistake, but mind you, it won't happen again Drannon. I'm not here for a wild fling. In two weeks, I'll be leaving, and I won't leave my heart behind. Got it?"

For just a moment, she thought he might argue. She was surprised by how much she wanted him to argue with her. Instead, he gave her a wicked smile that promised he wasn't giving up that easily, and held his arm out. "You know, riding is a hands on experience. You'll never learn the joy if you can't relax and let yourself welcome the wild nature of it."

She gave him a glare that was met with loud masculine laughter as he led her in to dinner. In her heart, she knew she was already ankle deep in a puddle of trouble. Drannon Russo made her weak. His nearness seemed to set her body on fire with a fever that could only be cooled by his touch. How she was going to survive without getting burned was anyone's guess.

~ ~ ~ ~

Drannon's heart was racing in his chest, and he could probably split wood with the erection in his pants. He'd never held a woman in his arms who made him feel so out of control. His ex-wife had turned him on, but it was in a younger, innocent way. The lustings of a teenager for the girl next door.

Lacy, however, lit his fuse like a firecracker, and he nearly exploded too quickly. As disappointed as he was to hear that she felt guilty over their hot make-out session, he wasn't about to let her brush him off that easily. What happened between the two of them was nothing short of epic, and it deserved his full attention.

The moment they entered the dining room, the hair on the back of his neck rose, and he felt something primal stir in his chest. All of his brothers were already seated and the interest they focused on Lacy was more sexual than his inner caveman could tolerate.

"Well, hello." Roman jumped to his feet and stepped closer to Lacy. Too close for Drannon's comfort. When she accepted Roman's offered hand, and he pressed his lips to her knuckles, Drannon very nearly growled out loud. "I'm Roman Freemont, but you can call me Romeo."

"Nice to meet you. I'm Lacy Denvers." She giggled, and Drannon touched her waist to gently guide her away from his younger brother. Before he could put much distance between the two, Hawke was at his elbow brushing past him to reach Lacy. He offered his hand, but thankfully, refrained from putting his lips on her.

"I'm Hawke Kapshaw, and Lacy, you are absolutely beautiful."

Leave it to Hawke to be blunt. Lacy gave the blonde man a brilliant smile, and pressed her hand to her upper chest. "Wow, thank you. Um, back at'cha handsome."

Before Hawke could take advantage of the compliment, Vin reached over the table and offered up his hand, "And I'm Vin. I might not be as handsome, but I've got them all beat in size." The wink Vin gave her put a clear exclamation mark on his double meaning, and Drannon rolled his eyes.

Lacy's eyebrows rose, and she gave him a confused look. "I thought Marilyn said there were no other guests here right now?"

"Vin's not a guest," Drannon explained, "He, and the rest of this pack of wolves are my brothers, and co-owners of the ranch."

"Oh, I—" she paused and then looked from one man to the next frowning. "Russo, Kapshaw, Freemont...you're brothers?"

"Yes ma'am." Roman said, snagging her hand once again, this time pulling her away from Drannon. He held her chair as she settled in and then swiped the seat right next to her, leaving Drannon to take the chair at the end of the table on her left. "We're not blood, obviously, but Abe and Sera Crawley took us all in when we were kids and gave us a home. We more or less adopted each other."

Lacy nodded, smiling, "That makes more sense. I was wondering why none of you looked alike."

Drannon took a moment to really look at his brothers like he hadn't in years. Hawke with his shoulder length blonde locks and blue eyes looked Scandinavian next to Vin with his olive complexion and dark blue eyes. Roman's hair was sandy brown, and it fell in feminine waves to his shoulders. Women couldn't seem to resist his hazel eyes, and charm, hence his nickname. Of the four, Drannon was the oldest, but he only had a year up on Vin, and considering what Vin had lived through, he figured they were more than equal in experience. Even with all of their physical differences they shared many personality traits born and bred in the foster system cycle and the rebelliousness of young boys. He respected them and took pride in the fact that they looked to him as the patriarch of their family now that Abe was gone.

"...always wanted to learn how to ride a horse, so I booked the trip never even considering what the weather would be like." Lacy's voice interrupted Drannon's thoughts, and he turned back to catch the threads of conversation.

"Where are you from originally?" Hawke was asking, leaning forward to scoop food onto his plate as he listened with rapt attention.

"Chicago is where I've lived for the last two decades, but before that I lived wherever my dad's job took us. I was born in Wichita, Kansas."

Drannon couldn't tear his eyes off Lacy. Her movements were graceful and sleek, and with her long neck and slender build, she reminded him of a gazelle. She'd be beautiful astride a horse with her crimson hair billowing behind her.

"Hey D! You still with us?" Vin snapped his fingers in front of Drannon's face, and he startled, frowning.

"I'm right here, what do you want?" he snapped at his grinning brother.

"I've asked you three times to pass the potatoes, but you were making googly-eyes at Lacy here and must have missed it." Vin said, winking at their guest again. For a moment, Drannon considered punching the smug look off of Vin's face, but the pink blush on Lacy's cheeks and the embarrassed way she fidgeted helped him restrain himself.

"Here," he said, shoving the bowl of spuds in Vin's direction, "I was going over monthly numbers in my head not making googly-eyes."

The lie tasted bitter on his tongue, and the look Vin shot him proved it sounded just as sour, but the conversation resumed around him. As usual, Roman made the woman laugh, while Vin made her blush, and Hawke romanced her. Drannon was beginning to think perhaps she'd forgotten he was there, when she suddenly reached for his hand. It was clenched in a fist on the table, but the moment her soft skin brushed over his, he shivered.

"Are you okay Drannon?" she asked, concern tinting her question.

Warmth filled him, and he forced his grip to relax so that he could turn his hand and weave their fingers, pressing his palm against hers. "I'm great. So, you were explaining that you booked the trip months ago, but why didn't you postpone your trip when you realized there was going to be snow?"

"Snow?" she asked looking down at her plate with a frown before she shrugged. "Honestly, I didn't bother to check the weather when I packed my bag and headed for the airport. I lost my job right before the holidays, and I've been a bit out of sorts since then. I'm trying to build my own business, but it takes a lot of work and more capital than I have available. Right now, I'm waiting to hear back from a big client about a marketing campaign I presented to them. If it tanks…well…I don't know what I'm going to do."

"So, you're in marketing?" Hawke's attention was less romantic and more serious now. "Do you, like, plan advertising and tell businesses how to grow?"

"Sort of, yes. I'm in marketing, but I specialize in graphic design. Logos, advertisements, that kind of thing. It depends on what the business needs. This company needed a whole new branding of their product after a recall last year, so they were more willing to think outside the box. Most companies find a team and stick with them until they aren't making money anymore. It's hard to get in with big corporations." Lacy explained.

"Do you know how to create a website?" Hawke asked, and Drannon immediately recognized where his brother was going with the conversation.

"Hawke, no. She's a guest, that's all," he said firmly, shaking his head at his brother.

"But—"

Lacy was frowning at him now, "I'm sorry, I don't understand. Do you need a website for something?" When Hawke hesitated, she prodded him further, "Because the answer is yes, I do know how to create one. Is this for the ranch, or for yourself?"

Hawke gave Drannon and apologetic smile, and then proceeded to explain their lack of business sense to the only woman who'd lit Drannon's fires in years. Damn it, now she was going to think he was a stupid cowboy who couldn't build a business.

Cursing his luck, Drannon pulled his hand away from Lacy, who barely seemed to notice as she spoke animatedly with Hawke, and now, Vin and Roman were in on the conversation. The four of them were excitedly coming up with ideas for some form of advertising campaign that would get the ranch noticed by adventure seekers as well as families.

"Whoa! Wait a second. We're not your average vacation destination, guys..." Drannon cleared his throat and corrected himself. "...and Lacy. We're offering therapeutic stays to veterans with PTSD as well as lodgings for foster children. We can't just invite everyone in America to come spend a weekend in the midst of that."

Lacy frowned, and nodded, "You're right, that's not the best environment for a B&B."

"A B&B?" he asked.

"Bed and Breakfast. It's the term used for a place that's generally less sophisticated than a five star hotel, but offers a homier, more comfortable atmosphere and usually a great experience. I haven't seen much of the ranch, but what I have seen has been fantastic. The ad that I saw when I booked my stay said that you guys were a dude ranch, but it feels more like a B&B now that I'm here. I think you have a great opportunity to build up the guest side of the ranch, but not if you're more focused on the therapeutic side."

"Why can't it be both?" Vin asked shrugging. "I don't understand why we can't market it as a B&B for people who need space from the world to get their head on straight. Foster kids, convicts, vets with PTSD, vets who are homeless and trying to get back on their feet."

"I'm sorry...convicts?" Lacy asked, looking wary all of a sudden. Drannon's stomach tightened in a knot.

"Yeah, but not the seriously violent ones. Just the guys like us that have been through the ringer and need to regroup when they get out." Vin answered casually.

Just like that the temperature in the room dropped by twenty degrees as Lacy stiffened in her chair. "Guys like you?" she whispered. For a moment she sat frozen in her seat, but when she stood it was clear by the expression on her face that she was going to run, and Drannon felt sick to his stomach.

"Lacy, wait, let me explain—" he was up and following her out of the dining room before she responded.

"No, that's okay. Hearing that I'm vacationing in a house full of convicts is enough of an explanation or me. That really should have been on part of the information I was given when I booked the stay, you know? I was right the first time when I said this isn't the best environment for a B&B." She made it to the bottom of the stairs before he caught her arm and spun her to face him.

"Wait a damn minute. Listen, you don't know my story, but suffice it to say I'm not a convicted felon. I was wrongly accused of a crime, but ultimately proven innocent. I did, however, have to spend a few months in jail while awaiting the evidence that set me free. Vin has been to jail, but it was for protecting a woman. Hawke was a distraught kid who made mistakes, and yes, he did some time. Romeo has always been able to charm his way out of trouble so he's barely spent twelve hours in lock up, but I'm sorry if you feel like we hid something from you. It's not the best way to advertise if we state on our fliers that we've all been arrested before."

Snorting out a nervous laugh, she shook her head and crossed her arms over her chest, "No, I'm sure it's not." They were both silent for several moments, and he was afraid she was going to make another escape. He wanted her to understand, but he wasn't ready to spill all of the beans yet. If she took off without giving him time, well then, maybe she wasn't the woman he'd hoped. Relief filled his chest when she finally met his gaze again, "I'm sorry. I jumped the gun and freaked out over nothing."

"Yep you did, but I might be willing to forgive you." He smiled down at her as he moved a step closer. He could see the pulse in her throat flutter faster, and she inhaled sharply as he drew close.

"Thank you, I think." Her eyes were locked on his lips. He licked them, and nearly groaned when she imitated the move.

"Lacy…" That was all he managed to say before their lips connected and his brain stopped functioning. What was it about Lacy that short circuited his logic? Molding his body against hers he couldn't have pinpointed who moved first; all he knew was that the two of them were equal partners in their coming together.

She parted her lips accepting his seeking tongue into the hot cavity of her mouth, and ran her fingers through his dark hair as he slid his hands up her spine to the back of her neck holding her tightly against him. He could feel her breasts against his chest, and her soft, sweetly feminine scent filled his nose, consuming his senses. Pressing her backwards against the railing, he broke their kiss off with a curse when she stumbled on the step.

The fire in her chocolate-brown eyes was roaring with need and called out to his inner caveman. How would she react if he threw her over his shoulder and carted her off to his bed? Before he had a chance to make his move, she darted under his arm and up the stairs leaving him standing at the bottom in stunned silence.

Well, hell.

Chapter 5

Lacy spent the remainder of her first night on the ranch buried under blankets in the super soft bed, reading her book. She was able to avoid Drannon the next day because she slept late, and he apparently had to help do something to prepare the cattle for the coming snow. According to Marilyn, North Dakota had been having an unusually mild winter, but that was coming to an end. Although the weatherman had announced that the snow was coming in slower than expected, the first round of it was still going to be here at some point in the next twenty-four to forty-eight hours, and thus, in the midst of her trip. Lacy was disappointed that she would have to wait for the weather to turn before she would be able to learn to ride a horse, but no one had control over Mother Nature. It was more important that she have this personal quiet time to herself. Time to reflect and be sure about the direction her life was going.

There were only a couple ranch hands around the barn during the day, and she assumed the rest of the men were with Drannon in the fields. They all seemed to be exceptionally busy, so she just waved hello and moved on. She took a couple of carrots outside to Toto after telling Marilyn how much she enjoyed meeting the horse, and spent a good half hour chattering at him while he tried to ignore her.

She'd already set up her laptop in the study and spent way too much time checking her social media accounts and praying that an email from the dog food people would pop up. As much as she was enjoying the quiet, she was also finding herself bored and a little lonely. It surprised her how excited she was to see the guys when they came stomping into the ranch house as the sun was setting late in the afternoon.

"Going to have to light the fire tonight and veg out after all that." Roman was saying as he peeled the layers of warm clothing off and hung each piece on a designated hook.

"Yeah, but we'll all sleep easier knowing the herd is covered if we get three feet like they're saying." Drannon answered.

"Three feet?" Lacy asked, drawing their attention. "Of snow?"

"Well, I doubt he meant we were all being blessed with a third leg, but I suppose anything is possible." Drannon's playful answer did nothing to slow the building panic in Lacy's gut.

"But, if we get three feet of snow, it will take weeks to melt." She was already imagining being unable to get back to Chicago in time to accept the job she'd worked so hard to get. If she couldn't meet with them in person like they'd specified would they still want her?

Drannon was nodding, and Roman and Vin were looking at her like she was nuts. Why didn't they see the severity of this forecast?

"How am I supposed to learn to ride a horse if I can't even walk to the barn to see one?" Her frustration seeped into her voice giving it a whiny tone that made her cringe. She didn't mean to sound like a temperamental child, but she hadn't taken a vacation in years, and of course, when she finally did, she screwed up and booked it in the midst of a blizzard.

"That's why we rarely get guests between December and April. Some years we've been snowed in for weeks. We've gone days without power even," Drannon answered with a shrug as though what he'd said was no big deal.

"Why would you live here if you know you could be buried under snow all winter?" She asked, noting that Vin's face was taut, like he was holding back his laughter. Drannon didn't seem flustered by her at all, and Roman was outright grinning at her.

"Can't beat the view." Was the only answer she got, as the men finished putting up their winter gear and moved farther inside the house leaving her to trail behind.

"Don't worry Red, we've got four wheel drive trucks, so we'll make sure you can get home on time. We can't promise you'll get to trail ride like you wanted to, but you'll get to enjoy a real North Dakota blizzard." Roman was trying to cheer her up, but it wasn't going to work.

She felt like a brainless twit for booking her trip based on a 2 x 3 advertisement in a tiny travel magazine. It had seemed ideal last summer when she spotted the ad, but now it seemed like a nightmare. All of her reasons for wanting to spend a Valentine's Day birthday by herself seemed insignificant now. She was well and truly screwed.

"Okay, so what do you guys do when you're snowed in for days or weeks?" She followed them into the living room where Roman immediately gestured for her to sit next to him on the sofa, and Drannon went to the massive stone fireplace to build a fire. Vin flopped down in an oversized armchair and propped his socked feet up on an ottoman.

"Chess, checkers, backgammon and poker." Roman answered with a wink, and she stared at him blankly.

"Seriously?"

He nodded, "Yep, most of the time the power goes out in a big blow like they're predicting, so the generators have to take over. We try to conserve their power by turning on only the things necessary like lights and kitchen appliances. Until then we'll be playing video games."

"So, no TV? No internet?" She was trying hard to wrap her mind around the idea of being trapped in the house with four scorching hot cowboys and nothing to do. If the snow held out too long she'd never be able to resist Drannon, and she'd end up in his bed for sure.

Drannon finally rose from the fireplace and turned to her. "Lacy, it will be just fine. We'll get some snow and have to stay in for a bit, but then everything will start to melt, and you'll have a chance to get out there and see for yourself how the ranch works if you want to. Romeo is just trying to freak you out."

"It's working. I never thought I was claustrophobic before, but the idea of not being able to leave the house if I wanted to…"

Roman patted her leg, "Think of this as a spa vacation. We have a steam shower, a Jacuzzi tub, great food, a few good bottles of wine, and I can even hook you up with a deep massage if you're interested." He wiggled his eyebrows at her, and she felt her frown slipping as her tension eased.

Vin threw a pillow at Roman laughing, "It's deep tissue massage, you jackass, and I'm sure Lacy has better taste than that."

Drannon wasn't exactly frowning, but he didn't look pleased with Roman's teasing, and she felt the need to up the ante just a bit at his expense.

"A spa, huh? Does that mean I get to lie around in my bathrobe all day long while someone pampers me?" she joked back, glancing up to find Drannon staring back at her with a look so hot she felt burned to the core. His jaw clenched, and she swallowed hard. He looked like he wanted to eat her up, and she was tempted to let him.

He shifted his stance and nodded. "Absolutely. Think of this as your home while you're here, anything you want or need, just ask."

The fire in her belly sizzled at the underlying desire in his tone. There was enough sexual tension crackling in the air that Lacy could almost taste it. Roman and Vin were both looking at her with wide smiles, but neither one had the heat that their brother's gaze held. Turning back to Drannon, Lacy gave him a smile before accepting a glass of wine from Marilyn who'd just bustled in. "Then I will just have to make the best of this blizzard by forcing myself to take a long, hot bubble bath tonight I guess. Poor me."

Her joke broke the tension, but Lacy noticed that Drannon's eyes stayed on her as the conversation shifted to things that still needed to be taken care of before and during the storm.

She loved the camaraderie the brothers shared, and she stayed quiet listening to them all banter back and forth. Apparently, Roman was a regular Lothario in Wrangler's and boots, which made his nickname Romeo all the more accurate. Vin seemed to be the tough guy of the group; there was a raw sadness behind his eyes that tugged at her heart. The way they spoke about him, Hawke was clearly the youngest member of the boy band, and he was extremely intelligent. He joined in the conversation easily when he came in from the cold, and she found herself deep in a conversation with him about the explosion of social media and its impact on the way businesses advertised when Marilyn called them for dinner.

As they took their seats tonight, Marilyn joined them, and Lacy took the opportunity to make her apologies to the guys for her behavior the evening before.

"No worries, Red." Roman said waving his hand like he was wiping a slate. "We were all foster kids so we're used to being judged by people. It rarely hurts anymore. Besides, you didn't jump the first plane back to Chicago, so we figured Drannon must have set you straight." He winked at his older brother.

"Drannon cleared my misconceptions, yes, but that doesn't mean I don't owe you all an apology. We all have pasts, and you've clearly worked hard to put yours behind you. I respect that." She said, looking at each man in turn. Vin flushed a bit, and Romeo preened, but Hawke wouldn't meet her eyes. In fact, he seemed downright uncomfortable with the conversation.

"Now that you've soothed your guilty conscience, can we eat?" Drannon asked gruffly. She bit back a retort, and gave a sharp nod instead. There was something about this rugged cowboy that both intrigued her, and riled her up all at once. She couldn't decide if she wanted to jump his bones, or punch him. Where had the deliciously seductive man from yesterday gone? Why was he being so short with her today? Perhaps her rejection had actually hurt him more than she'd thought.

Dinner conversation was occupied with questions from Marilyn about her life back in Chicago, but she carefully avoided questions about her family. These guys had had it way tougher as kids than she had, and it wouldn't be right to whine about her motherless childhood.

When the chatter came back around to her plans for the future, Hawke seemed determined to convince her to come to work for the ranch. No one else jumped on the bandwagon, so she figured it was a pipe dream for the younger guy. It didn't matter much, she couldn't accept any kind of position with the dog food account hanging in limbo right now. That kind of money and the opportunity were too much to walk away from.

Even with a steady stream of tension between her and Drannon, Lacy had to admit she was enjoying herself with this bunch of people. The guys were genuinely friendly, if not flirty, and Marilyn was a true gem. It had to be wonderful living in a place like this full-time and be surrounded by family.

Her thoughts strayed to her own awkward family dynamic, and a heavy sadness filled her chest. She'd never had the close bond with anyone that these four men shared, and yet she and her father were blood relatives.

A warm hand on hers stirred her from her wallowing, and she looked up to see Drannon watching her with concern. His thumb stroked the skin on the back of her hand soothingly, but thankfully, he didn't ask questions. She wasn't ready to spill her heart out to virtual strangers, even if they were the most welcoming people she'd ever met.

~ ~ ~ ~

"So am I supposed to shoot that guy or just stun him?"

Drannon sat in the corner of the family room with a farm equipment catalogue on his lap, mindlessly turning the pages as he paid more attention to Lacy and his brothers than what he needed to be doing. After dinner, Hawke and Roman had convinced her to give the Xbox a try, and she'd been nestled between the two men for the last two hours. Jealousy stirred in his chest at the easy way she'd accepted their gentle touches while they helped instruct her on the game. It wasn't as though they were being inappropriate, but then again, Roman Freemont wouldn't know appropriate if it bit him in the ass.

"If you just stun him, he'll shoot you in the back when you walk away," Hawke was saying, just a hint of frustration in his tone.

"What if I stun him and then shoot him?"

"That wouldn't be very sportsmanlike," Hawke argued.

Lacy giggled, "Since when is war about sportsmanship? I thought I was supposed to be killing the bastards?"

"Bloodthirsty wench. I like it!" Roman threw his arm around her shoulders and tugged her into his body. The fact that he did it didn't bother Drannon as much as the fact that Lacy let him, and didn't pull away. Enough was enough. If he wanted a chance to seduce her, he was going to have to get her away from the dynamic duo.

"Hey Lacy, I'm going to walk out to the barn to check on Dorothy, do you want to walk with me?" He spoke loudly and dropped the catalogue in the chair as he rose.

She tossed a frown his way before turning back to the TV. "Who's Dorothy?"

"She's one of our pregnant mares," Hawke offered, never tearing his gaze from the guerilla hunters darting about the screen amidst gunfire.

Lacy began to giggle again, "You have a Toto, and a Dorothy? Good grief, someone has a *Wizard of Oz* fetish."

Roman winked at her as he took her controller. "Not quite a fetish, but it is Drannon's favorite movie from childhood. Did he introduce you to Munchkin yet?"

She shook her head, and Drannon could feel his cheeks heat when she looked his way.

"Munchkin is a milking cow," Vin explained, entering the room with a big bowl of popcorn and dropping down onto the floor next to the sofa where the other two were sitting. "Although she doesn't produce much milk these days."

"Drannon's had her for more than a decade," Roman said, clearly intent on obliterating Drannon's manhood in Lacy's eyes.

"Aw, that's so cute! I'd love to meet Dorothy and Munchkin, but isn't it going to snow?" Lacy moved around the couch in his direction.

"Yep, but the animals don't give a damn. Someone still has to trudge out to the barn to check on them." Drannon said, reaching for her hand and drawing her away from his family. The sudden urge to have her alone was so strong he nearly swept her off her feet. She barely resisted, and he managed to get her into the foyer. When she reached for her shoes, he asked, "Are those the warmest ones you have?"

She frowned down at the sneakers in her hands. "Yeah, I didn't bring snow boots because, as we've established, I didn't plan well for my trip. I'll be fine. It's not snowing yet, so at least my feet will stay dry."

Shaking his head, Drannon put his own boots on, and then reached to help her into her coat. She gave him a funny look, but slid her arms into the sleeves and zipped up. "I don't think anyone has ever held my coat for me." She murmured so softly he wasn't sure he heard it.

"Then you're clearly not dating the right men."

Her eyes widened slightly, and she whispered, "Clearly."

The tension between them grew thicker when he reached for her hood, and carefully pulled her braided hair over her shoulder so that he could situate the covering correctly. He noted the increased rate in the pulse at the base of her throat matched the thumping of his own heart, and he hurried to release her before he did something stupid. His lips tingled with the need to kiss her, but if he kept pushing her, she was going to run straight back to Chicago before he had a chance to convince her to stay.

The reality of his own thoughts made him tremble slightly as he was putting his hands into his gloves. Was he really considering asking a woman he'd just met to move in with him? What the hell was he thinking?

"Do we need flashlights or anything to get to the barn?" Lacy asked. He looked up into her beautiful, brown eyes, and recognized the desire lurking in them. She wanted him, but was desire enough to base a relationship on? Maybe she'd consider a fling while she was visiting. The thought brought a bad taste to his tongue and he grimaced unintentionally. "Sorry, I didn't know I wasn't supposed to ask that."

"Oh, no, I wasn't frowning at your question. Sorry, I was lost in my own head." He hurried to assure her. "No, we don't need flashlights. After thirty years on this ranch I'd have to be strung out drunk to have trouble finding the barn, even in the midst of a blizzard. Luckily, it's just dark out."

He held the door for her to exit first so that he could attempt to peek at her denim clad ass as she went, but her coat concealed it.

"So, how did you come to be on the ranch?" she asked conversationally as they turned so that the icy wind was at their backs, and hurried towards the barn.

"My mom OD'd when I was eight. I didn't have any other family that could take me in." He answered shortly, trying to focus on slowing his pace so she could keep up with him. They reached the barn doors quickly, and he pulled one open just enough so they could slip through into the warm shelter. Like a cocoon, it enveloped the two of them in the scent of hay and animal, and Drannon breathed it in deeply. This was his favorite place on the entire ranch, and he let himself take a moment to enjoy the fact that Lacy was standing next to him.

"I'm sorry about your mom. I can't imagine what it was like to go through that when you were so young," she said, her eyes reflecting the sincerity of her words.

"I won't lie, it sucked, but her death ended up being the best thing that could have happened to both of us. She found peace from the never ending addiction, and I found Abe and Sera Crawley."

Lacy gave him a small smile as she pushed her hood off. "Tell me about them. Everyone speaks so highly of the Crawleys. I wish I'd had a chance to meet them."

Reaching for her hand, he led her down the main aisle of the barn as he started to speak. "Abraham Crawley was as old-fashioned as they come. He believed in raising boys to become men, and girls to become ladies. He wasn't a mean man by any measure, but he was tough. I think we all needed that. Tough love goes a long way with kids who haven't had any sort of center point in their lives. Lots of kids passed through Crawley Creek Ranch, but a few of us stuck. Sera was the mom I dreamed about having when I was a young kid. She cooked, and sang, and rode a horse as well as any man. I've always imagined finding my own Seraphina Crawley and having a love as deep as hers was with Abe. When I was a kid, I thought they were angels sent by my mom to take care of me like she couldn't. Mind you, I didn't have those same golden beliefs as a teenager, but then, what teen enjoys having boundaries and discipline?"

His comment got the desired giggle out of her, and he smiled over his shoulder. She was so beautiful when she smiled, he stumbled over his own feet and cursed sharply.

"Are you okay?"

He felt his cheeks heat with embarrassment, but he took a chance when her face reflected only concern for him. "I'm fine. It's just when you smiled at me, I forgot how to walk for a moment."

Her intake of breath was followed by a sweet sound that rocketed straight through his body to his groin making it throb uncomfortably. Her lips were parted in an O shape that brought to mind all sorts of dirty things he had no business thinking.

"I'm beginning to think they've given the wrong man the nickname "Romeo." She teased.

Drannon slid his arm around her back, and pulled her closer, "I'm not Romeo, but I can admit when I find a woman attractive. I'm not going to play games with you Lacy. I want you. I want to finish what we started yesterday. I want to touch you and taste you, and hear you screaming my name when I take you to my bed." He paused to let that sink in, enjoying the flush that filled her cheeks, and the way her chest rose and fell with her labored breathing. "If you want me to back off, just give me the word."

Silence grew heavy between them, and the temperature rose by twenty degrees. Drannon held his breath as he waited for her to turn him down, but she just licked her lips smiled.

"So what are you waiting for, Cowboy?"

The words made his cock rock hard in his jeans, and he groaned before dropping his mouth to hers.

~ ~ ~ ~

Scorching hot fire blazed through Lacy's body the moment they connected. She loved feeling the rasp of the day's beard growth against her cheek, and the rough material of his brown coat against her fingertips. Each sensation made her already sensitive nerves raw, which made his kiss that much sweeter. Once again, her brain fried under the onslaught of his passion, and she fought to keep her knees locked underneath her.

He expertly swept his tongue between her lips, tempting and teasing her into a playful kiss that led to nips and deeper, hungrier kisses. His hands slid down her back to her ass, and she could feel him tugging her coat higher so that he could cup her curves in his palms. When he finally reached his goal, she sighed with pleasure at the contact. She knew the size of her own butt, and he had massive hands that seemed to fit it perfectly. All she wanted was for him to… A moment later, she had her wish, as he lifted her and carried her a couple feet away to a stack of hay bales.

The new position gave his hands more freedom, but the layers of warm clothes between them hampered their amorous endeavors. She giggled against his lips when he struggled with the zipper on her coat, and when he finally released it and started to push it off her shoulders, she shivered.

"Shit." He grumbled, "This isn't right. I won't take you for the first time in the barn like this. You deserve better."

She smiled when he sweetly kissed her forehead and pulled her warm coat back over her shoulders. The tender action eased the last of the doubts she had about this vacation fling. If she had an option, she might pack this cowboy up and cart him back to Chicago with her, but since she didn't, she'd just enjoy the time she had with him.

"We got a little carried away anyway. You're supposed to be introducing me to your friends." She jerked her head toward the deeper interior of the barn, and he smiled.

"That's right, we still need to check on Dorothy. Come on, we'll make it quick, and then I'll show you how we like to keep warm in North Dakota winters." He led her to a stall that held a pretty golden brown horse with a black mane. As he opened the stall door, he began talking softly. "Hey pretty lady, how are you this evening? How's that baby doing? You still look beautiful, yes you do."

Lacy watched from outside the stall as Drannon approached the horse and ran his big hands gently over her coat to her belly. He continued to pet Dorothy soothingly the entire time he was checking her over. Once he was content with her condition, he gestured for Lacy to come inside.

"Lacy meet Dorothy. The lady of Crawley Creek."

She grinned at the introduction, and held her hand out as the horse nuzzled her, inhaling her scent. Dorothy seemed to approve of her because she gently bumped Lacy's knuckles with the bridge of her nose in a gesture that clearly requested a pat. The hair between the horses eyes was softer than a baby's skin, and Lacy sighed. "You're certainly a beautiful lady, Dorothy. It's lovely to meet you."

"Dorothy is the oldest mare we have on the ranch, and she's produced several of our best horses. I have a feeling this will be her last pregnancy though. This one's been hard on her." Drannon ran his hand under the rounded belly of the animal just as Dorothy decided to snuff at him. "I hear ya, girl, but I'm not willing to give you up just on the chance we can get another winner out of you."

"A winner?" Lacy asked.

"Her first son won a world championship. She's produced several offspring that have won various contests actually." Drannon explained.

"Wow. I can see why she'd be proud to keep having babies then." Lacy laughed when Dorothy nudged her again as though in approval.

"Well, like it or not, I've got to protect the lady of Crawley Creek, so this is her last baby." Drannon said with one last pat to Dorothy's rump. "Come on, we'll say hi to Munchkin and then get back inside. I can hear ice on the roof."

Lacy paused in surprise and realized that she could hear what sounded like rain pattering against the metal roof of the barn. "Should we wait and come back tomorrow to see Munchkin?"

The look Drannon gave her as he secured Dorothy's stall door could have melted iron. "Lacy...baby, I have a feeling that once I get you in my bed I won't be letting you go so quickly. And besides, the ice will be followed up by snow, which I will be even less likely to get out of bed for."

She followed his lead and met Munchkin the cow before they ran for the ranch house. The ice was coming down hard, and it pelted her cheeks painfully. By the time they reached the house, her shoes were soaked through, and she was glad to be inside the warmth.

Drannon noticed her wet feet the moment she tugged her shoes off, and he dropped to his knees while still wearing his coat to cup her foot in his big hands. Her wet socks hit the floor as he began rubbing her toes vigorously to warm them up. "Damn it, I should have found you a pair of boots to wear. I'll be pissed at myself if you end up with frostbite."

"Hey," she reached out and cupped his cheek in her palm. "You didn't know it was going to start sleeting while we were out there. I'm fine, I promise. I'll go up and soak in a hot bath to get my blood flowing again and be good as new."

"Not without me you won't," he said huskily, kissing her hard before he got back to his feet and shrugged out of his coat. Lacy hurried to follow, stripping her winter gear and thrusting it haphazardly into the storage cubby in her haste. In record time, the two of them were racing up the massive staircase barely acknowledging Marilyn's hello as they swept by her on her way to bed. Lacy considered feeling embarrassed, but she was a grown woman, and she had a hot cowboy who wanted her. There was no need for self-recriminations. All that mattered right now was fulfilling the driving need for Drannon that rolled in her belly.

Chapter 6

Desire overrode Drannon's need to be a gentleman, and at the top of the stairs, he scooped Lacy up, throwing her over his shoulder as he continued on down the hallway to his bedroom. She gasped at the impact of his shoulder on her stomach, but the caveman act turned her on more than she wanted to admit. Just knowing he wanted her so much he couldn't wait was doing a number on her libido.

She was correct in her assumption that his room was the one at the end of the hallway with the double doors, and she barely got her head up to look around before he was putting her down on a massive bed. The room was richly masculine in decoration and surprisingly modern compared to the rest of the home. His bed was black and chrome as were the end tables on either side, and she caught a glimpse of a black metal ceiling fan when her back hit the mattress and before his body blocked out her view when he followed her down.

He pressed open mouthed kisses to her jaw and throat, sucking slightly with each kiss and making her drip with anticipation. Bath forgotten, she began sliding the buttons of his shirt open, one at a time until she could see the dark curls of chest hair over his pecs. She leaned forward just enough to press a kiss against his collarbone, and giggled when he let out a rumble of appreciation. Drannon tugged her shirt off to reveal her breasts and tweaked a nipple gently. Lacy arched her back to press her breast further into his hand, aching for him to grab it hard and have his way with her. She wanted the desperation back, not this gentle, sweet lover.

Lightly nipping at his lips, she grabbed the two flaps of his shirt, and pulled as hard as she could, pleased with herself when the last couple of buttons went flying. He chuckled and grabbed her hands.

"Feeling a little needy, huh? Patience never killed anyone, sweetheart."

"Easy for you to say, you're not the one dripping on the bed! And I am not talking about the water from outside." She winked and he groaned, pressing his mouth to hers in a deep kiss that seemed to sizzle all the way to her stomach.

When they broke apart she got her first good look at his well-muscled chest and abs, and she nearly drooled in delight. He looked like he'd been carved from stone by Michelangelo himself. Each ripped ridge made her pussy clench, and she skimmed her fingertips over his skin memorizing the map of his physique. Black ink drew her attention to his left side, and she tugged at his arm to get a better look.

"What does it say?" she asked, frowning at the words imprinted on his golden skin.

"Growth before pride, in Italian." He answered. "My life's motto."

He didn't elaborate, but she made a mental note to ask him about it later. He was delightfully distracting as he began tugging at her remaining clothing. It only took another moment for him to strip her jeans and panties from her body, leaving her blissfully naked to his hot gaze. When he paused his movements to stare down at her, she wiggled impatiently and tugged him down on top of her again. She spread her knees a little wider, and he shifted, sliding his groin into the V of her thighs. His jeans were rough against the sensitive skin of her pussy, but she rocked against him regardless. Running her hands under his open shirt, she felt hard muscles rippling under heated skin, and heard her own moans of appreciation as he captured her nipple with his lips.

This man was built better than any she had ever seen, much less touched. Hard work and long days seemed to create muscles like etched granite. Her mouth watered to taste him, but she couldn't reach with his face pressed between her tits. Feeling frustratingly needy, she tugged at his bicep, hoping he would lift up a little. Instead, he bit her nipple making her squeal in surprise at the sharp pain.

"Hey!"

His dark head lifted enough to nail her with his gaze, "What's the rush? I want to take my time and make love to a beautiful woman. Do you have somewhere better to be?"

Lacy flinched at the question, "No! There is nowhere else I would rather be. I just want to show you how crazy you're making me. You've got me pinned down so that I can hardly touch you."

Drannon shook his head at her, "No, you were in a hurry to get your orgasm started. Well, Miss Denvers, you will learn that, in my bed, we do things at my pace."

He reached up to release her hair from its braided coil, and when it finally relaxed out of the tight binding and spread out in a red wave around her head, she was pleased at the awe on his face. Lately, she'd been considering cutting it off to give herself a new look for her new life, but seeing how much pleasure Drannon got out of it made her glad she'd held off.

"Your hair is stunning,"—he paused to press a kiss to her nose, and then grinned—"as are you. Now roll over."

He was up and off her before she could respond, and she laid there, staring at him in surprise. "What?"

"Roll over. I want to see if your ass looks as good out of those tight jeans as I've imagined."

There was no way Lacy could have denied his request. She rolled, rising up onto her knees and elbows so that her ass was up in the air pointing directly at him. If he wanted to see her ass, then she was going to ensure he got the best possible view of it. Her hair hung over her shoulder pooling on the bed beside her.

"Fuck me, that's beautiful." His words sent a shiver of heat down her spine, and she glanced over her shoulder just as he opened the zipper on his jeans. The fat, purple head of his cock was poking out the top of his black boxer briefs, and her mouth watered at the pearly drop of fluid resting on the tip.

Within moments he was completely nude and crawling up onto the bed behind her. His lips and whiskers tickled the back of her calf as he pressed butterfly-soft kisses to the tender skin of her right leg from ankle to knee. She dropped her head to rest on the bed when he continued his slow journey up the back of her thigh. When he reached the curve of her ass, he paused, and for a moment, she thought he might give her what she wanted and delve between her thighs. Instead, he dropped his mouth to the back of her left ankle and repeated the process up the back of her other leg.

For several minutes, the only part of him touching her was his lips, and it was one of the most erotic moments of her life. When she felt his hot breath finally dance over the split of her ass, she moaned into the bedspread.

"See what I mean, sweetheart? Let me do this my way; you won't regret it." His hands flattened on her rounded ass cheeks and spread them apart, opening her completely to his view in a way that no one had ever seen her before. She could feel her own juices dribbling down her thighs as he examined her. "You have the sweetest pink pussy. I wonder if it tastes as good as it looks."

His tongue felt enormously thick as it parted her pussy lips from the hood of her clit all the way to her perineum, and she gasped at the contact. His hum of approval answered the question he posed, and she felt her knees slide farther apart giving him more room. He took full advantage of the access as he used his tongue and lips to explore her labia and clit, moving over the sensitive flesh in a teasing dance.

Digging her fingers into the mattress beneath her, she thrust back in time with his movements, craving release. Every time she got close to the edge of orgasm he pulled back, making her wait until she was panting and desperate.

"Drannon, please!" the words broke from her throat along with a sob of need, and she clenched around the two thick fingers he pumped in and out of her passage.

He rose up to his knees, and she felt his cock prodding against her pussy lips before he pressed past her vulva and into her tight channel. He went about half way before stopping to let her adjust, and she whimpered, pushing back against him.

"Easy, I don't want to hurt you."

She was so frustrated and needy that she heard a growl burst from her throat just before she slammed back against him, surprising them both. "You won't break me! Fuck me, please God, just fuck me!"

Her plea seemed to be his trigger because Drannon began pounding his hard cock into her needy pussy, slamming into her so hard, that she had to grip the bedspread to keep from sliding across the bed. His fingers tightened around her hips, holding her in place for his own purposes. She loved it. Every moment of his passion matched the depth of her desire, and she ached for more.

She could hear her own voice babbling, moaning, whimpering, and begging for more, but she wasn't even thinking straight. Every thrust brought new sensations to her already electrified body, and she clenched her cunt around him as she soared over the edge of climax. Her knees collapsed out from under her, so that the only thing holding her up was his hands holding her against him.

Her spasming pussy milked his cock until he was groaning out his release as he filled her full of cum, and slumped over her back. For several moments they both just rested there, trying to bring their breathing and heart rates back under control.

When Drannon finally rolled to the side, he reached out and brushed her long hair away from her face so that he could see her, and smiled. "If it's worth doing, it's worth doing right, sweetheart, and I do believe we did that right."

"God help me if that was the wrong way," she said with a giggle as she turned onto her side to face him.

His cum was leaking out of her well used pussy, reminding her that they hadn't used protection, and she bit her lip.

Immediately Drannon noticed and sat up to look at her better, "What is it?"

"This is a little awkward, but I know I'm clean, and we didn't use a condom…"

She paused as he considered her words. When her meaning clicked he looked startled. "Oh shit, you're asking…yes! I'm clean! I'm not going to try and lie to you and say I haven't had sex, but it's been a long time. Are you on the pill?"

She nodded feeling relieved and stupid all at once. She was usually a very responsible person, and yet somehow she found herself lying in bed with a virtual stranger, his semen growing sticky between her thighs. Wouldn't her dad be proud?

This whole vacation was turning upside down and backwards on her. Wanting to learn how to ride a horse had brought her to this new place where she seemed to have completely lost her mind and ended up in bed with a cowboy. It was like some sort of eighties romance novel, and she already knew that a piece of her heart would be left behind in North Dakota when she went home.

~ ~ ~ ~

Drannon held his breath as he watched a myriad of emotions cross Lacy's face. After such a beautiful, intimate moment, he wanted to keep the warm glow they'd created between them for as long as possible. Maybe if he'd slowed down to think about protection they wouldn't be sitting there in awkward silence.

"I'm sorry. I'm an ass." He said, pulling away with the intention of going to clean up. She stopped him with one hand on his arm.

"You're not an ass. I'm sorry. I guess I just spaced for a moment. What is it you called it? Lost in your head? Yeah, I got lost in my head for a minute. I'm not upset. We're both adults, and we were responsible." The way she rubbed her thumb over the dark hairs on his forearm made his cock twitch, and he gave her a sheepish smile.

"I'll make it up to you in the bathtub." Rolling her way, he pushed her off the bed, catching her up in his arms as he did so that she never hit the ground.

"You still want to take a bath?" she gasped in surprise.

He nodded, "Of course. I'll use any excuse to keep you naked and wet."

The sound of her laughter echoed off the tile bathroom as they entered followed by a gasp of awe. "Holy smokes!"

Lacy scrambled out of his arms and made her way around the bathroom, taking it all in. Drannon looked around at the massive master bath through new eyes and realized it really was an impressive sight. Abe and the boys had remodeled the master bedroom a dozen years before as a gift for Sera. They'd knocked out walls and incorporated two smaller bedrooms creating a luxuriously oversized master suite. The bathroom was as large as the bedroom Lacy was using while she was on the ranch, and next to it was a door that led into a combination dressing room and office. Sera had used the room for clothing, but she'd also kept a soft chair near the big windows that faced the front of the house to use while she read a book or crocheted a new blanket. The chair still sat in its original place with its original faded and worn upholstery because Drannon couldn't bring himself to get rid of it. He sought its comfort when he needed to reflect, or think through something serious.

After thoroughly exploring, Lacy turned back to him, beautifully naked, and cocked her hip. "What does a single cowboy need with a two-person jetted bathtub?" she asked with an arched eyebrow.

"It's been there for years, and to be honest, I've never used it myself. I think this is the perfect time to break it in." He turned on the tap.

Out of the corner of his eye, he noticed Lacy shiver in the cooler air of the room, and he reached for her, pulling her between his legs as he sat on the edge of the tub. Her breasts lined up perfectly level with his face, and he pressed his cheek against their plush softness. She didn't object, in fact, she wrapped her arms around his head and held him close, the moment of intimacy deepening. They held that position for the few minutes it took for the tub to fill, then she stepped back to let him up.

"Where are the towels?" she asked, retrieving them when he gestured to a linen cabinet. She came back stroking the soft green cotton like she'd stroked Dorothy earlier. "These are fabulous. Where'd you get them?"

He shrugged, "I don't know. You'd have to ask Marilyn. She handles all of that stuff for us since Sera died."

"I clearly need a Marilyn in my life." Lacy muttered under her breath. He laughed as he helped her into the tub.

"I'd be willing to share her with you, but she's not leaving the ranch, so that only leaves one alternative," he said playfully. Her beautiful body sank down into the steaming hot water and she sighed.

"She'd love Chicago, but I have to admit, this place has its perks."

Drannon was glad Lacy's eyes were closed because it gave him a moment to just survey her. Like a mermaid, she lounged gracefully against the white porcelain tub, her rich red hair drifting on the lapping waves around her. It clung to her breasts, and darkened into a crimson stain that reminded him a bit of rubies.

"Are you joining me, or just watching?" Her question was soft, and her eyes were still closed, but Drannon could hear the amusement in her tone.

"I was just wondering how long it'll take us to dry your hair after our bath. I plan on getting you pretty wet." He stepped into the water and sat down so that he was facing her. The two seats were angled perfectly for the two of them to have a conversation while they bathed. Her delicately shaped knees poked up out of the water as she relaxed against the backrest, her eyes drifting shut.

"It will take awhile. It's really thick."

"Why do you always keep it braided?" he asked stroking his fingertips over her calf under the water.

Her eyes cracked open just a bit, and she shrugged, "It's easier to keep under control when it's in a braid, and it attracts less attention. You'd be surprised how many men are drawn to a woman with long hair just because they have some fantasy about it."

"I have a few fantasies about it," he teased, and she grinned.

"We'll have to explore them later."

"So if it's such a hassle why do you keep it long? Wouldn't it be easier to just cut it?"

"I've asked myself the same question a million times." She paused, and then slid deeper into the water, "I suppose I could blame my own vanity, but if I'm honest with myself I think it stems from the fact that my father hated dealing with my hair when I was little. As a single dad he struggled to help me keep it washed, and brushed, and styled so he regularly made me cut it. When I was old enough to take care of it on my own, I promised myself I wouldn't cut it unless *I* wanted to."

As he listened to her talk, he pulled her foot up onto his chest and began rubbing the arch, enjoying her sigh of pleasure. The more he stroked her soft skin, the more she relaxed. He wouldn't be surprised if she fell asleep. He wanted to ask her more questions about her father, and why she was raised by a single parent, but she seemed skittish about the subject, so he let it drop.

"You're hired," she murmured sleepily.

"Excuse me?"

"You're hired as my personal masseuse while I'm on the ranch. I can't imagine any other cowboy having better hands than you," she teased, and he growled softly.

"You better not be imagining any other cowboy's hands on you, period, or I'll have to break his fingers."

Her eyes popped open and she laughed. "You'd hurt a man just because I imagined him touching me?"

"Damn right." He squeezed her foot then pulled her hard so that she slipped from her comfy spot and dipped under the water. When she came up sputtering, he moved her into his lap, pressing his firm cock up against her hot opening. "I might be a gentleman ninety-nine percent of the time, but there's still the one percent piece of me that's a jealous asshole. You're mine, damn it."

She wiped the water from her face, and stared back at him. Irritation followed quickly by surprise lit up her beautiful chocolate brown eyes, and he thought for a moment she was going to let him have it. What he didn't expect was for her to drop her mouth to his and press closer. This time *she* demanded, and he let her have her way with him. Her tongue stroked across his teeth before she nipped his bottom lip, and curled her fingers into his hair and held him close. When she finally paused for a breath his balls were throbbing and they were both panting.

"Damn," he whispered.

"I like it when you get jealous; it's fucking hot. I'll make you a promise that I'm yours"—she paused and started to say something before shaking her head—"as long as I'm here."

Drannon wanted to argue that she never had to leave, but this wasn't the best time for it, so he reached up and wrapped his fist in her hair, pulling her lips back to his. He wanted to make sure she knew what she would be giving up when she left.

With Lacy lashed to him by her hair, he slid his other hand beneath the water to her spread pussy lips. She wasn't as slick as before because of the water, but her clit was swollen, and she squirmed against his fingers when he stroked her. He loved the soft sounds of pleasure she made when he touched her, and he promised himself that he'd hear that sound a hundred times before she went back to Chicago.

While he was lost in thought, Lacy took matters into her own hands, literally. She wrapped her fingers around his hard shaft and pointed it in the direction of her welcoming cunt. Realizing that she was a woman on a mission, he accommodated her by rocking his hips upward while she sank down, swallowing his length with her body. Heavenly heat surrounded his cock, and they both groaned as they came together.

"Fuck, you feel good," he murmured.

"So good," she agreed, rolling her hips in a figure eight pattern that nearly made him come. Her devious grin assured him that she knew what she was doing as she repeated the move again and again, driving him mad with pleasure.

"Woman, if you don't stop I'm going to—" his words were cut off when she repeated the motion and laughed at his corresponding groan.

"Going to what? Hold me down and fuck me? Please do."

On the verge of explosion, Drannon took her at her word and grabbed her hips in his hands, rising from the water with her still attached. She wrapped her long legs around his waist and looped her arms tightly around his neck. He moved the five steps from the water to the vanity where he gently placed her ass on the cold marble countertop, and took her wrists in his hand, holding them high above her head.

"Just remember, you asked for it," he said, slamming his hips forward and filling her completely. She was immobile in the position he held her, but he had all the freedom he needed to fuck her hard and deep.

Electricity seemed to crackle in the air, as her cries of pleasure echoed off the tiled bathroom walls, and he responded with grunts and groans of his own. He whispered dirty words, and encouragement to her as she climbed closer to climax. He wanted to watch her face, and see her eyes when she exploded around him, but at the last second, a zap of that electrical fire between them hit him hard. His vision when dark just as he emptied his balls deep inside of her spasming pussy.

Slumping against her, he could hear the racing rhythm of her heart in her chest as she tried to catch her breath, and he let himself imagine that she was as full of emotion as he was.

"That was incredible," she whispered against his forehead.

"Damn right. Give me a bologna sandwich and a thirty-minute nap, and we'll take it from the top."

She giggled. "I don't think so, big boy. It's been years since I've had sex, much less good sex. My lady parts are going to be aching tomorrow."

Drannon lifted his head and smiled down at her. "Well then, I'll just have to kiss them better."

He helped her off the counter, and held her against his chest until she steadied herself. He loved how she fit against him, and the sweet way she nuzzled her nose into the gap of his collarbone. How could she not see how perfect they were together?

"I better dip back in the tub and wash off before I head for bed. I don't want to wake up with sticky thighs."

He let her take care of herself while he cleaned up as well and went back in the bedroom. He fully intended she would sleep in his arms, but when she came out of the bathroom, she went directly for her clothes.

"Where do you think you're going?" he snapped, his voice angrier than he meant it to be, and he cringed inside at the look of surprise on her face.

"The lilac room. I can't be here in the morning for Marilyn to find, Drannon." She tugged her jeans on. "It wouldn't be appropriate."

"She walked in on us earlier in the study, I'm sure she's adult enough to deal with it," he argued.

"That's not the point. I don't want my stay here to be awkward."

"Are you ashamed of what happened between us?" he asked, anger and disappointment burning in his chest. "Don't want anyone to see you with a mangy old cowboy?"

"What? That's ridiculous. I just don't want anyone to get the wrong idea. I'm only here temporarily, so there's no point in people whispering about us." She wrapped her long hair in the towel she'd been wearing when she came out of the bathroom. Drannon was tempted to drag her back in the bed. He wasn't ready to ruin whatever they had started though, so he just nodded, swallowing the bitter taste of rejection.

"All right, then. Sleep well." Rising from the bed, he went into the bathroom and shut the door behind him, effectively putting a wall back up between them.

Chapter 7

The next morning found Lacy awake with the sun. Just as she had hoped, it looked magnificent streaming through her windows as it crept over the eastern horizon. From her view of the sky through the crack in the curtains, there wasn't a cloud in sight. Perhaps the weather forecasters were wrong and the snowstorm hadn't actually been as catastrophic to her vacation as she feared.

Tugging on a pair of yoga pants and a sweatshirt, she made her way downstairs for breakfast, smiling when she heard Marilyn singing in the kitchen while she cooked. Cinnamon scented the air making Lacy's mouth water.

"Good morning."

The husky deep voice startled her and she stumbled on the second to last step of the stairs landing hard on her ass. "Ouch!"

Two massive arms slid under her shoulders from behind, and Drannon lifted her to her feet as he came down the last couple of steps. "Damn it, I'm sorry! I didn't mean to scare you."

She rubbed her now bruised backside and turned to face him. Her breath caught in her throat as he stared back at her with concern and wariness in his brown eyes.

"It's okay, just a bruise. Good morning." His eyes traveled down her arm to her elbow where it disappeared behind her as she rubbed her ache. She felt a blush creep up her cheeks. Scolding herself, she tipped her chin and forced a smile. "I was just going to get breakfast."

"I really am sorry. I was surprised to see you awake so early. After last night, I was afraid you'd be in avoidance mode." He gave her a wry smile, and she sighed heavily.

"No, not at all, and I'm sorry about last night. I didn't mean to hurt your feelings. I'm just not ready for everyone to know about…well, you know. I'm not normally the type of girl—"

His eyes narrowed as he interrupted her, "I never thought you were. Like I told you, this isn't a regular occurrence for me, either. There's just something about you that draws me in. Like a bee to honey, or a moth to a flame."

"Or a spider to a fly," she murmured, dropping her gaze.

Marilyn's soft singing suddenly stopped, and Lacy looked up to find her in the doorway of the dining room watching the two of them as they stood at the bottom of the stairs. Her blue eyes were full of concern telling Lacy that the tension in the air wasn't just her imagination.

"Is everything all right?" Marilyn asked, rubbing her hands on the towel she kept over her shoulder.

"Absolutely. I was just following that delicious smell down the stairs and slipped. Drannon helped me up, and he was making sure I wasn't hurt." Lacy said with all of the false cheeriness she could muster.

Marilyn's smile turned into an O of concern. "I do hope you're all right! We're so far from town, and with the snow we got already, taking you to a doctor would be awfully tough. I can call Starla down on the Rocking Tree ranch and see if she can come over. She used to be a nurse at a big hospital."

"No, no. That's not necessary. I bruised my pride a little, that's all. You said it snowed already?" she asked, frowning.

"Yes ma'am, about ten inches or so. The next round should start this evening, and Marty on The Weather Channel said it's going to be a hefty one." Marilyn said, nodding as though what she was saying was normal. Lacy couldn't imagine getting this kind of snow regularly. How did people manage to get anything done in the winter months?

Determined not to let the snowstorm or the liaison with Drannon ruin her vacation, she smiled at Marilyn. "So, are you going to tell me what that sinful cinnamon smell is, or keep me in suspense?"

"It's French toast, and I promise you've never had better. This was my mama's recipe for it. Of course, back in her day they called it 'nun's toast', but it's the same rich, sweet treat. Have a seat. The other boys and I have already eaten, so dig on in." Marilyn disappeared into the kitchen to get something leaving Lacy to take a seat at the table full of food with only Drannon for company.

Silence reigned as the two began filling their plates. Lacy's first taste of Marilyn's french toast melted on her tongue. She closed her eyes as a moan of pleasure slipped out. When she opened them, Drannon was watching her with amusement lifting his lips.

"Good, huh?" At her nod, he began eating, too. "No one cooks better than Marilyn. The woman is a saint. We've had many guests try to steal her away, but thankfully, she says Crawley Creek is where she wants to be."

"I wish I had her talent. I can make a mean egg sandwich and heat soup from a can, but I'm no chef. It might've helped if I'd had a mom to teach me like Marilyn did." She regretted the words the moment they fell off her tongue, and she nearly choked on her next bite of food when Drannon froze in place.

"Why didn't you have a mom?"

It was the question Lacy avoided at all costs. The guilt rose up to overwhelm her, and she fought back tears as she took a quick swallow of milk to get the food down her throat. Drannon couldn't have known that her mother was the one subject she hated talking about, especially since she was the one who'd brought it up.

"My mom died giving birth to me."

Drannon's fork clattered when it dropped to his plate and he inhaled sharply, all of his attention on her. "I'm so sorry sweetheart, I shouldn't have asked."

Lacy took a deep breath before she looked at him. To her surprise there was no pity on his face, only concern for her. "Thank you, but it's been thirty years tomorrow, and I never knew her, so I can't dwell on it. She had a weak heart, but she wanted children desperately. The doctor told her she should terminate the pregnancy because she might die having me, but she wouldn't do it. She never even told my dad there was a risk. She died just a few moments after holding me for the first time."

"I can't imagine the kind of hell your father must have gone through. Gaining a daughter and losing a wife in the same day. He must be a strong man."

"I think he was at one time, but losing my mother must have changed him. When I was young he was a good dad in the sense that I had everything I needed, but he shut himself off from a lot of things because he didn't want to risk getting hurt again. He always seemed a bit too cold, and standoffish. By the time I was in high school we didn't have much of a relationship." She turned back to her food now that she had won the battle over her own emotions, and to her relief, Drannon followed suit.

"Does your dad live in Chicago, too, then?"

"No, he moved to Des Moines a few years ago because of his job. I see him every now and then, but we lead separate lives. I'm sure I'll hear from him tomorrow for my birthday, but then, it's unlikely I'll hear from him again until Father's Day unless I seek him out. We're just not close." Shrugging, she tried to play off the hurt that saying those words out loud caused her.

For years, she had wished for a different kind of relationship with her Dad, but he couldn't forgive himself—or her—for her mother's death. She could remember wanting to scream at the top of her lungs, "Why can't you just love me, too?" but she never did, because she was afraid of the answer she might get from him.

"Tomorrow is your birthday?" Drannon looked surprised, "On Valentine's Day?"

Lacy blushed again, and took a sip of milk before nodding. "It's not a big deal. I've never really celebrated it. Between it being the anniversary of Mom's death and a stupid holiday created by the gift card industry to empty our wallets, it just never felt like a good day to me."

Drannon reached out and covered her hand on the table. "Everyone should celebrate the day of their birth. If your mom wanted you to live so badly that she was willing to sacrifice her own life, well then, I would guess she would want you to enjoy every passing year and celebrate it."

Lacy returned his smile, but shook her head, "Thank you, but really, it's not a big deal. I prefer to just get it over with."

Drannon took a few more bites quietly watching her, before he spoke again. "You're lucky to have either parent. Sometimes I wonder if my mom overdosed on purpose. I mean, it wasn't like she had a great life…" He paused and Lacy felt tears burn her eyes at the sad look on his face. "If it weren't for Abe and Sera who knows where I would've ended up. They gave me a home and a life, and when I needed it ten years ago, they gave me a second chance."

Lacy heard the underlying pain in his words when he spoke about his adoption. He might love the Crawley family, but clearly, he also had a few unresolved feelings about being an orphan. She turned her hand in his and linked her fingers with his, enjoying the heat of his palm at it pressed against hers.

"What do you mean, they gave you a second chance?" she asked, knowing instinctively that this had something to do with the time he spent in jail.

A wrinkle appeared on Drannon's forehead, and a haunted look filled his eyes. "In another lifetime, I went to college and got my degree in finance. I moved to Dallas and worked for a Fortune 500 company for almost five years before everything went to hell. I was accused of embezzling millions of dollars, and I was arrested. My dumb ass chose to sit in jail rather than call Abe and Sera and tell them I'd been arrested. So, I stayed in jail and got a public defender."

Lacy shook her head, "And the attorney proved you were innocent?"

"No. After several days, the PD finally came in and told me about the so-called 'evidence' they had against me. It turns out my boss was the one who committed the crime, and he picked me to pin it on. The PD told me there was no way he could prove it, so I should take a plea deal."

"Are you fucking *kidding*?" Her outburst took them both by surprise, and it brought a smile to his face.

"Just wait, the good part is coming. At this point, I realized that if I didn't give up my pride and call the Crawleys for help, I was going to be spending a lot of time in jail for a crime I didn't commit." He paused, and squeezed her hand. "That was the toughest call I've ever had to make in my life."

"I bet. So what did Abe do? I can't imagine he was very happy with you."

Drannon laughed. "No, he wasn't, but he was a very proud man, so he understood where I was coming from. He brought in an expensive defense attorney who hired some sort of technical genius to pull the information from the computers at the company. It wasn't a quick process, but they were able to prove without a doubt that the transfers weren't made by me, so the case never went to trial, and I was released."

There was a deep silence as Lacy absorbed all of the new information he'd revealed. He'd survived so much more in his lifetime than she had, and yet here she was pouting about not having a mother. It strengthened her somehow to know that he'd not only come through all of that, but thrived as he reached the other side.

"Thank you for telling me all of that. I'm not sure I could have started my life over the way you have, and I have to tell you, I'm impressed. You're a strong man, and I'm sure Abe and Sera would be proud of how you've turned out."

The warmth finally returned to his brown eyes, and he nodded, but emotion seemed to choke him up.

"You're also very right about what you said, from what I know about my mom she wouldn't be happy with me for not celebrating, and she would be heartbroken at how far my father and I have drifted apart. I don't see it getting any better if I take the next step in my career and stay in Chicago. Dad hates the city, and he was relieved to be moving to Des Moines because he could live farther away from the crowds."

"What's the next step in your career?" Drannon picked up his fork with his left hand and began to eat awkwardly. It took her a moment to realize he was doing so because she held his right hand and he was right-handed. When she attempted to tug her hand away he held her firmly and even began drawing little circles on the back of her hand with his thumb. "Tell me, what big plans do you have for your future, sweetheart?"

"Well, if I land that marketing campaign I put a bid on, it will mean at least twelve months of steady work, but it will also mean I'm tied to Chicago because the company insists on biweekly meetings for status updates." She was getting full, so she leaned back in her chair, flipping her long braid over her shoulder. Drannon's eyes followed its movement, and she was reminded of how his fist felt in her hair. A shiver ran over her skin and she clenched her thighs together.

"When will you know if you got the contract?" he asked, his voice slightly deeper now.

"Any moment. They said they would have an answer by the fourteenth."

"Wow. Tomorrow is a big day for you all around. Why exactly is a beautiful woman secluding herself on a ranch in the Dakotas for

Valentine's Day? You should at least be going out on a date to a lovely dinner in the city."

Lacy snorted and then laughed. "I don't date. Well, I mean I have dated, but every time I find a guy who seems nice on the outside, he turns out to be boring or nasty to the core."

"I'm not sure if that was a dig at me or not, but I'm going to assume you're generalizing because it makes me feel better," Drannon said frowning at her.

Lacy laughed out loud. "No, it wasn't directed at you, but you did ask."

"It's sad to me that you're so cynical about relationships." He spoke softly, pushing his plate away as he finished his food.

"How old are you?"

Drannon looked surprised, "Thirty-eight last November, why?"

"At thirty-eight years old, society would say that you should be married with children, but you're a single man who owns a ranch with his three brothers and relies on a housekeeper. You can't tell me that you have no angst in your past from women."

Drannon was still holding her hand in his, but now he leaned forward and pressed a kiss to the back of it. "You're right. I was married once. I was nineteen and she was my high school sweetheart. I truly had no idea what forever meant back then, but I cared about her. She moved to Texas with me, but as it turns out she met someone else a couple of years into our relationship and divorced me. It took some time, but I finally realized that I never really loved her the way a husband should. I married her because it was what I thought I was supposed to do, and when she found someone who made her happier, she left."

"See, it proves my point. Relationships and love just aren't worth the headache. I have my career and some friends, and that's enough for me."

"Is it? The woman I took to bed last night was full of passion and so hot she nearly scorched the sheets with me. How can you tell me that a cold bed at night and the lack of companionship is what you really want? I know it's not what I want."

Lacy stared back, unable to break their eye lock. What was he trying to say? They had only spent a few hours together, so it was impossible that he was interested in a serious relationship with her.

"That's exactly what I'm saying. I want to build my business, have my freedom, and damn it, I want to learn to ride a horse."

Drannon frowned then a slow smile spread over his face. "It's going to snow more in a few hours, but I'll be damned if you'll leave this ranch without fulfilling one of those goals. Layer up, sweetheart, it's gonna be cold out there. You have ten minutes."

He stood and swiftly pressed a hard kiss on her gaping mouth before she could respond, and headed out of the room. A spark of excitement lit in her chest. He was going to let her ride a horse.

Chapter 8

Toto looked much larger with a saddle on his back.

Lacy swallowed hard as she watched Drannon tugging at the straps holding the saddle in place. She really did want to learn how to ride, but now that she was standing here in the moment it seemed like a much bigger challenge.

"Okay, up you go." Drannon turned and looked at her expectantly, before he laughed loudly. It took her a moment to realize he was laughing at her.

Tightening her jaw and jutting her chin out defiantly, she glared at him. "You aren't a very good teacher. What am I supposed to do?"

"We haven't even started the lesson yet. For that, you have to be in the saddle." He reached his hand out for her and waited until she took it. "You're going to put your left foot in the stirrup, and then push off the ground with your right leg. Hold the pommel here, and pull yourself up. Once you're high enough, just throw your right leg over the saddle. Toto is a veteran. We use him to teach all of the kids who come through the ranch."

"Ha. Ha," she snapped as she secured her left foot in the stirrup and followed his instructions. Drannon held the reins in one hand, but he still managed to palm her ass as he helped lift her into the saddle. It was awkward at first, made even more so by the fact that she wore yoga pants under her jeans to keep warm, but she felt a burst of exhilaration rush through her as she stared down at the ground from the saddle. "I did it! Oh, my God! I did it!"

Drannon chuckled, and patted her thigh. "Yes you did. Now, I'm going to lead for a few minutes until you get your seat, once you're comfortable I'll give you the reins. A horse takes its direction from the rider, so if you're nervous, he'll get fidgety, but if you stay calm and in control he will do whatever you ask. Okay?"

Lacy nodded and focused on relaxing as she swayed with the saddle. It was everything she had hoped. The icy cold wind stung her nose and cheeks, but she felt warmer inside than she had in years. The freedom she'd craved while ensconced in her tiny city apartment was finally in her grasp. She loved the gentle sway of the saddle underneath her, and the creak of the leather as Toto fluidly made his way around the fenced ring. He seemed completely indifferent to her presence on his back, but her heart filled with adoration for the massive beast. She reached out with one hand and stroked his mane, the rough hairs scraping across her soft palm. It reminded her of the bristles on Drannon's jaw, and she shivered as a wave of desire coursed through her.

She didn't understand why she was so attracted to him. Sure, he was sexy as sin, but he was also a country man—raised in the wilds of North Dakota and determined to spend his life there. She was a city girl with big dreams, and she had absolutely no clue about living on a ranch. Why was she playing with fire?

After several laps around the corral, Drannon passed her the reins and stood back to watch her. She felt more comfortable the longer she sat in the saddle, and she laughed with pure joy.

"What's so funny?"

"I'm riding a horse! I'm really doing it! I have dreamed about doing this since I was a little girl, and I'm finally doing it. Thanks to you." She gave him a smile and giggled again when two pink spots appeared in his tanned cheeks.

"All I did was saddle him up. You're the one who has natural talent. You're a born cowgirl, Lacy."

"She sure is." Roman's voice came from behind her and she twisted around to find that she had an audience watching her from the barn doorway. Embarrassment clawed at her until she realized they were all grinning and giving her the thumbs up or some form of verbal encouragement.

"Looks like she was born in that saddle." Vin said, spitting something into the snow. "Any chance you want a job cowgirl? We could always use a new hand."

"I'm not cheap," she teased back.

"Women never are!" Roman called.

Her laughter was her only answer as she followed Drannon's directions, and climbed out of the saddle. His hands held her firmly about the hips, and her ass pressed against his chest, then abs, then zipper as he lowered her to the ground. The warmth of his body felt good and she realized she was shivering.

"We'd better get you inside. It's going to snow again soon." He tugged her hat down tighter around her ears. "I wouldn't want you getting sick while you're on vacation."

Lacy glanced up and realized that there was a dark grey shelf of clouds moving in from the west. It was rapidly covering up the stark blue sky, and it looked like the weatherman might be right.

"Okay, but I want to help put Toto away first. He deserves that for being a good ride." She declared.

Drannon laughed and winked, "And do I get a treat for being a good ride?"

With a cocky sway of her hips she spun toward the barn. "Maybe."

The other guys had gone back to their business or headed for the house by the time Drannon and Lacy had Toto unsaddled and rubbed down. Drannon assured her that the horse was content with his regular feed as a treat, since he hadn't worked overly hard carrying her around in circles.

"I know he didn't have to exert himself, but he was my first," she said, knowing exactly how it sounded. The barn had gone quiet as everyone sought out the warm comforts of home, leaving her and Drannon alone with the animals. She reached out and ran her hand over the back of his canvas coat. Being this close to her dreams made her giddy, and her body was rippling with excitement that needed an outlet.

He caught on quickly to her desire, and he spun her around, capturing her lips for a passionate kiss. His tongue swept into her mouth, and one of his hands held the back of her head in place. When they were both panting, they broke apart and stared at each other. "You sure can kiss, cowboy."

His lip curled up, and his black eyebrow rose, "Thank you. I'd love to spread you out in the hay and make love to you right now, but you'd better haul that cute ass into the house and get yourself a hot bath. I wouldn't want any parts of you to freeze off."

He palmed one of her breasts through her layers, to emphasize his meaning, and she laughed pulling away and heading into the house. Even if it snowed for the rest of her trip, and she wasn't able to do it again, she knew that she would never ever forget the feeling of sitting in the saddle with the wind whipping over her and Drannon watching her. Just hearing him tell her how well she did left her feeling ten feet tall as she made her way upstairs.

She spent the rest of the morning in the bathtub and then reading her book on the chaise in the study. Someone had lit a fire in the fireplace, and she was warm and cozy. She must have dozed off, because the next thing she knew a pair of warm lips were easing her awake.

Drannon knelt on the floor in front of her, his fingers stroking over her temple and cheekbone as he stared down at her.

"I came inside to warm up and found an angel sleeping in my study."

She smiled at his compliment before kissing him back. "Your nose is still cold, so you haven't done a very good job of warming up."

Lust sparkled in his eyes, and he grabbed her knee, jerking suddenly to spin her body from lying down to seated with her knees on either side of him. "You know the nice thing to do would be to help me warm up. They say body heat is the fastest way to do that. Wanna get naked and test the theory?"

Lacy laughed when he wiggled his eyebrows playfully. "What if someone walks in on us again? Marilyn seems to have terrible timing, and all of your brothers are inside now because of the weather."

"It's after noon. she'll be napping for a couple of hours. My brothers are playing video games, so they won't bother us. But I could be convinced to move this upstairs if you're interested." He took her hand and pressed it to the hard ridge beneath his jeans, and her mouth went dry. She knew it was probably the worst thing she could do, but she wanted him again. While she had the chance, she wanted to feel totally free for the next couple of weeks. If that meant riding a horse—or riding a cowboy—she wanted to experience it all.

Squeezing gently, she leaned forward and ran her tongue over his bottom lip. "Do you think you can handle me, without getting thrown, cowboy? I've been told I'm a natural rider."

His groan of appreciation was swallowed in a fierce kiss, before he shot to his feet and locked the study door in a lightning fast move that made her laugh.

"Anxious much?" she teased.

"Absolutely." He reached for her shirt and helped her strip it off. Once she was naked, she took over and attacked his zipper. He helped by removing his shirt, and she giggled when she heard buttons go flying again. At this rate, he wouldn't have any shirts left with buttons.

The moment she got her fist around his hard cock, she felt her stomach tighten and her mouth began to water. She wanted to taste him. Last night had been about her, but now she wanted control. Her tongue slid over the crown and she heard him moan.

"Shit, sweetheart, if you do that I'm going to embarrass myself."

"Shhh..." She blew air over the tip of his cock, "I want to. You can make it up to me."

Her mouth widened to take him as deeply as she could and he gasped.

"Holy shit! Your mouth is on fire! That's so fucking nice, baby."

Lacy hadn't given many blow jobs, but she was determined to give him the best experience she could. Being careful of her teeth, she pushed him further into her throat. She gagged and choked just slightly, and she realized that her gagging made his dick grow even harder in her fist, so she repeated the process, never pushing herself too far, but giving him the sensation of her throat closing around the head of his cock. Within a few moments, she felt a burning ache in her jaws and she released him, disappointed with herself.

Drannon didn't seem disappointed at all. He dropped to his knees in front of her on the couch, and shoved her thighs apart, exposing her dripping slit to his view. She had to brace herself on the edge of the cushion as he spread her pussy lips and began licking her in earnest. His tongue flickered over her clit making her twitch and moan, and he pushed one long finger into her and fucked her with it.

She rocked her hips towards him, begging for more, and trying to get him to stop all at once. She wanted to be full of him before she came.

"Drannon, please, fuck me!"

He hesitated and then pressed a kiss to the curly red hair of her mound before he stood again. This time, he was a little less stable as he toed off his boots and pushed his jeans the rest of the way off. When he was gloriously naked, he sank back to his knees and lined his cock up with her pussy. The thick head teased her clit and she whimpered.

"What do you say?" he whispered.

"Damn it Drannon," she cursed, trying to arch her body and force him inside of her.

"That's not the magic word. Say please, Lacy."

"Please Lacy!" she begged.

"Nuh uh." He dipped the tip of his dick into her moist opening and then pulled it away.

"Oh please Drannon. I need you."

"That's a good girl." He surged forward, filling her to capacity and making her cry out her need. "Tell me what you want Lacy. Do you want me to fuck you? Fill you? Make you come?"

"Yes! Yes, please! Holy hell!"

Her orgasm hit her hard and fast, and she cried out his name as she jerked against him, absorbing his weight. The delicious way they seemed to work together made each orgasm that much sweeter, and she nearly cried with the strength of emotion running through her.

"Now that we've worked some of that tension off, why don't we head upstairs to continue this," he murmured against her nipple.

"Oh, *now* you want to go upstairs?" she laughed.

"Yes, but I'll never come in this room again without remembering how it felt to have you begging me to fuck you." The emotions in her chest were reflected back to her in his eyes, and it stole her breath. Should she tell him?

Instantly, she tossed the idea aside and went back into her standard escape mode. "We're going to have to get dressed again."

"Nah, the boys are caught up in *Masters of Mercenary Mayhem* or something. I think we can get up the stairs without incident if we're quiet." He held his hand out to help her off the couch, but when she stood her knees buckled, and she fell against his chest.

His laughter joined hers as he led her out of the room and up the stairs, leaving their clothing behind. She was surprised when they turned towards her room instead of his bedroom, but she wasn't complaining. As long as they found a bed she didn't care whose it was.

He paused in the doorway and winked at her. "Climb on the bed sweetheart, I need to grab something."

She didn't have a chance to complain as he was gone in a flash leaving her naked in her bedroom doorway. With a grunt of frustration she did as he asked, settling herself on top of the pretty lilac bedspread with a couple of pillows at her back.

When he stepped back into the bedroom the first thing she noticed was the coil of rope in his hand, the second was that he locked the door behind him.

"What in the world?"

"I have to make sure I don't get thrown. You're looking at the best bull rider this side of Fargo. I have several belt buckles to prove it, but rope is necessary when breaking in a new ride."

He moved toward her with that fluid grace that she found so arousing, and she couldn't seem to move in protest. His hands slid up her arms to grip her wrists, and before she knew it, she was tied to the brass rails of the headboard. The rope was snug, but not too tight. If she struggled too much, she was sure to have rope burns on her wrists, but by the time she returned home, they should be healed. Giving him a mocking smile, she laughed.

"You think a little rope will tame me, cowboy?"

Drannon shook his head, "Nope. I don't want to tame you. I prefer you wild and wicked, but this will keep you where I want you while I fuck you until you scream my name."

His words made her hotter, and her body responded. Nipples that were already hard, grew even harder, skin that was already tingling now zipped with electricity. Desire blasted through her body as he rose over her and captured her nipple in his mouth, tempting and teasing her clit with the head of his cock.

He didn't take her yet and proceeded to make her crazy by rubbing his cock in the moisture between her thighs and teasing her from clit to asshole and back. He squeezed her breasts with his hands, and teased them with his mouth, occasionally biting down on one delicate tip just to hear her moan.

The need that was growing inside of her again was powerful, and she found herself grinding on him and pleading for mercy. Her fingers were curled around the rope, and her thighs were stretched to the limit on either side of his spread knees. She was completely open to him, and she found it fulfilling in an odd way. The fact that he wanted her so much made her feel powerful, even though she was clearly in the submissive position at the moment.

When Drannon finally finished teasing her, he gave her no warning before he shoved his cock into her pussy hard, bottoming out against her cervix making her cry out.

His thrusts were desperate, his face tight, and her body was on fire. Never in her life could she have imagined wanting someone so much. His powerful body looked backlit by the shadows of the gloomy skies outside, and in her mind's eye, it was epically beautiful.

They climbed to the top of a mutual climax. Like a musical crescendo she felt herself explode and heard her own lusty scream mesh with his groan of release. Never in her life had anything felt so right. His body collapsed onto hers, and he released her arms, pressing gentle kisses on each wrist before he rolled, taking her with him. She lay draped over his chest in the fading daylight and drifted to sleep to the sound of his heartbeat, surprisingly happy.

Chapter 9

A cool breeze over her body woke her several hours later. The room was dark but for the bright moonlight coming through the small crack in the curtains. Drannon lay on his side staring down at her.

"Wake up, Sleeping Beauty." He pressed a sweet kiss to her forehead.

"What time is it?" She snuggled into his chest, pressing her nose against his collarbone. His arms wrapped around her naked form, and she realized he must have tugged the blankets off her to wake her up. "It's dark, why are we waking up?"

"It's almost midnight, but I wanted to show you something." He hugged her tightly before he rolled her away so he could stand up. As she sat up she realized that he was already dressed, and wearing his boots, "Well, come on! The radar only shows a couple of hours before the snowfall starts again."

Grumbling as she climbed from the warm bed and got dressed, she followed him downstairs and through the quiet house. When he handed her her shoes and coat, she gaped at him.

"It's midnight; are you crazy?"

He laughed and knelt holding her shoe out for her foot. "Only for you, sweetheart. Let's go." She let him help her bundle up, puzzled as to what he could possibly want to show her in the middle of a nighttime snowstorm.

When he pulled open the front door, icy cold air and shock hit her simultaneously. Toto stood saddled and waiting in about two inches of fresh snow where the ranch hands had shoveled it clear just hours before.

"What is this?"

"We're going for a ride. Don't worry, it won't take long. I'll have you back in bed and warm soon." Drannon led her to Toto's side. The horse actually looked as perturbed as she would have been if she wasn't so moved by his desire to surprise her.

Drannon launched himself into the saddle and helped her up so that she was seated in his lap, caught between his groin and the pommel of the saddle. His hard cock pressed against her ass and, she wiggled a bit trying to ease away from it. "Pay no attention to him, he's been hard ever since a gorgeous redhead appeared on the ranch."

"He has good taste." She shivered a little, but she wasn't sure if it was from the frigid temperatures or the feel of him pressed so tightly against her.

Lacy struggled to take it all in. The snow that had already fallen glittered like diamonds in the moonlight. There were clouds to the east and clouds to the west, but at the moment, they were riding under a clear sky with a beautiful midnight moon. Stars filled the expansive black sky, making the whole world seem endless. It was stunning.

Content to let Drannon have the lead, and still a bit sleepy, she nestled into him and enjoyed the intimacy of the shared silence. After several minutes, he turned Toto and led him through an opening in the tree-line. The moon disappeared behind a cloud and the trees seemed to swallow up the warmth of their embrace. The beautiful environment was suddenly a bit creepier, and she twisted to frown at him.

"How far are we going?"

She couldn't see his face in the dark under the brim of his hat, but she could feel his hot breath against her cheek when he spoke. "Just another minute and we'll be there. Trust me."

For the first time, she realized she really did trust him. They'd only known each other for a couple of days, but she felt like she'd known him for lifetimes. Every story he and his brothers shared gave her new insight into the man who'd clawed his way from ruin more than once in his thirty eight years, and she found her respect and feelings for him growing.

How many times had she wished for a man in her life who was worthy of respect? Drannon Russo was one of a kind, and now that she'd had a brief taste of being treated like a queen by him, she wasn't sure any other man would ever live up to him.

"Here we are," he said, drawing her attention back to the present.

The sight in front of them brought a gasp from her lips, and Drannon chuckled. Spread out before her was the most magnificent view of a mountain range. A deep valley stretched for miles between the outcropping they stood on and the craggy steep slopes of the mountains. Snow covered every surface—trees, rocks, even a creek or river that ran off to the north of them.

"What is this place?" She asked breathlessly.

"Those are the Turtle Mountains. I wanted you to see the valley covered in snow. There isn't a more beautiful sight in the world, except maybe in the late spring when the forget-me-not flowers bloom. It's like a sea of pale blue buds, and the scent is heavenly." He paused, and it sounded distinctly like emotion cut off his words for a moment. "Very few people get a chance to see it like this. Usually, the snow comes down so fast that all access to the valley is shut down for weeks or months. I didn't have time to get you a gift for your birthday or for Valentine's Day, but I could give you this, and I wanted you to have a memory to take with you that was just yours and mine. I hope you aren't still mad at me for dragging you out of bed." He rested his chin on the top of her head, and she could feel the warmth of his breath against her cheek.

"Mad at you? How could I possibly be mad at you? This is the sweetest thing anyone has ever done for me. I love it. Thank you." A tear rolled down her cheek, and then another and another. The tears chilled her cheeks as they sat in peaceful silence. Drannon held her without asking questions, and she felt a comfort and security in his arms that she had only ever tasted briefly. His care for her touched her in a way she wasn't sure she would ever be able to describe.

After several minutes, it began to snow lightly, so Drannon set Toto on course back to the ranch.

"Why didn't the Crawleys legally adopt you when you were a kid?" she asked. She felt his chest rise and fall against her back with a big sigh.

"For a long time, it was because I didn't want them to." His answer surprised her, but she held her tongue hoping for an explanation. When he stayed quiet she shifted slightly to look back at him.

"What kid wouldn't want to be adopted?"

"You might be surprised. I was only meant to be on the ranch temporarily. When the social worker dropped me off, the plan was for her to find a more permanent place for me if she couldn't locate any family members. You know, they never even asked me if I had any other family." Underneath them, Toto huffed as if irritated by this bit of news. "I didn't, so it didn't matter."

"What about your dad?"

"Never knew him. I'm not even sure my mom knew who he was. She never talked about any other family, so I assume there wasn't any. Anyways, after a few weeks on the ranch, Sera asked me if I'd like to stay on. Vin was already here, and he and I clicked right away. She used to say we were like peanut butter and jelly—meant to be together. I'd never imagined having it so good as I did with the Crawleys, so I said yes. The state of North Dakota gave them guardianship, but I resisted starting the adoption process. I just wasn't ready to give up myself. I thought that if I was adopted it would mean I wasn't a Russo anymore, and my name was all I had left of my mom."

"Oh, my God, that's so sad." She murmured, tears pricking her eyelids.

"I know it hurt Sera and Abe that I didn't want to take their name, but they said they understood. Over time, lots of kids came and went, some stayed longer than others, but very few actually became part of the Crawley family, and none were ever legally adopted. The Crawleys didn't need adoption papers to be great parents; they just needed kids."

"Why didn't they have their own?"

"Sera couldn't. I don't really know specifically why, but I know she was barren. Abe agreed to start fostering kids shortly after they got married because Sera was a born mother. She was great at it. Small in stature, but she had an enormous heart" —he chuckled—"and that doesn't even compare to the size of her temper. I only remember her raising her voice to me a few times, because knowing I'd disappointed her hurt more than her anger. She was a great mom."

"Sounds like it." Lacy stopped asking questions, and just enjoyed the warmth of his arms around her and the sway of the horse. She was falling for Drannon. No doubt about it. He was everything a man should be. Tough on the outside, soft on the inside, and proud of who and what he was. Maybe he'd hit low points, but he managed to drag himself back to the top. She should take a page from his book and focus on getting her career back to the top instead of mooning over him.

"Tell me about your tattoo." She was determined not to let her heart delve into the scary world of love.

He shifted behind her, and one of his hands covered hers on the pommel, instantly warming them through their gloves. "I got it after I came back to North Dakota. It took me being in jail for those four months to realize that pride is dangerous. When I left the ranch to go to school in Texas, I truly thought I was moving on to bigger and better things. Somehow, in my mind, I associated this life—being a cowboy—with poverty and a lack of accomplishment. By the time I learned how good I had it, I'd fallen a long ways. I fought with my ex-wife over ridiculous material things because she hurt my pride when she left me. I refused to seek help when I needed it because I was embarrassed to admit I needed it. It took a lot for me to admit that the only way I would ever really be proud of myself is if I allowed myself to grow. So, growth before pride became my motto."

"And why is it in Italian?" she asked.

"Russo is an Italian last name, and the only thing I know about my lineage is that my mother was Italian. Her name was Elena Carlotta Russo, and other than that and her birthdate and death date I don't know much else about her."

"I'm grateful that I at least knew about my mom. There were times when I was young that I could get my dad started talking about the past, and it was really the only time he would smile. It almost always ended with him in a sad state of depression later, but it was worth it to see the memories through his eyes for just a minute." She didn't know why she was sharing such intimate details, but the more they shared, the more connected she felt with Drannon, and now that she'd tasted their bond, she craved it. "I had a doll that had long red hair when I was young, like ten maybe, and I used to pretend that my mother gave her to me because the doll looked a little like her pictures. I would talk to her, and tell her about my day…"

Drannon was quiet for a few moments, and the only sound echoing in the night was the rustle of the snow under the horse's hooves. "I stuttered as a child. Really bad. It wasn't until I moved to the ranch and found a stable environment that I was able to overcome it. I redirected my anger at my mom into fighting with the kids at school for awhile, but I remember Abe sitting me down after one particularly bad fight and giving me a talking to. He said, 'Son, if you're going to let those boys get you riled up because you say things in a unique way, then you're going to spend the rest of your life fighting. You need to stand up and accept that you were gifted with more abilities than they were. How many people are able to say things like you do?' "

Lacy couldn't help herself, she laughed at the image in her head and the interesting take on a stutter. "Well, that's one way to look at it."

"Yep, it served its purpose. I worked hard to tame the stuttering and the temper, and before long, I was the biggest kid in school, so nobody messed with me."

"I stayed to myself in school too. Not really because people picked on me, but more because they just weren't like me. I liked to read and listen to music, and I really preferred to be alone."

"So how did you end up in the big city then?" he asked.

"Work. I've been able to hide behind a computer, but in truth I was lonely."

"You don't have to be lonely anymore," Drannon whispered, pressing a kiss to her temple as they both fell silent again, lost in their own thoughts. Emotions swirled through Lacy's brain leaving her feeling off balance, and vulnerable. The closer she became to Drannon, the more she wanted to believe she really could have her cake and eat it too. He'd gifted her with a memory, but he made it so much more special by sharing himself with her. She'd never had anyone really want to just be with her for no reason other than they enjoyed her company. It was unsettling and fulfilling at the same time.

By the time they reached the front porch, she had her emotions back under control, and she kissed him soundly when he lifted her down off the horse.

"That was magnificent, Drannon. I've never had a better gift for my birthday. Thank you for taking me to see it."

"My pleasure, sweetheart. I have to put Toto away, but you go on in and get warm."

Lacy had a pot of coffee, and a couple of sandwiches made by the time Drannon came back in the house. He moaned with his first sip of the steaming drink, and he winked at her. "You know exactly how to keep your man satisfied. Hot coffee, good food, a pretty smile and hot sex. You're perfect. Can I keep you?"

Lacy laughed with him, but the question echoed in her head. They ate their sandwiches amidst mutual teasing and affectionate touches. Later, as they made slow, sweet love—in his bed this time—she felt pieces of her heart melting and binding with his. She couldn't imagine leaving the ranch after just a couple of days with Drannon. How much harder would it be in a couple of weeks?

As dawn was nearing, Drannon went to the kitchen to scrounge up another snack for them. When he came back, he informed her that Marilyn was feeling under the weather, and his brothers were handling the chores for the day, so they could stay in bed. Lacy watched the large cowboy as he settled a bowl of popcorn and a couple of sodas on his bedside table.

"Did you mean it?"

Drannon glanced up in confusion. "Mean what, sweetheart?"

"You asked me if you could keep me."

He froze in place and then slowly sank down to sit on the bed beside her with a heavy sigh. "Yes, I meant it."

Their eyes met and held, and she shook her head, "I'm not the relationship type. I don't know how to be...normal."

The corner of his mouth curled up in a sad half smile, "I'm not sure I would feel the same way about you if you were normal. You know, when I came back to the ranch from Texas, my heart was in pieces and I was angry. No, not just angry, I was bitter. Bitter over my ruined career, my wasted years, my failed marriage..." He paused, and pressed a kiss to her temple, "For years, I've hidden on this ranch from my hurt. I've had sex, but you are the first woman in decades who's made me want to feel more than just an orgasm."

"Drannon, don't fall in love with me," she whispered, biting down on her lip to keep from crying.

He huffed a despondent laugh. "Oh, if only it was that simple, sweetheart."

"It is that simple. This is temporary," she argued, struggling to keep her own emotions walled off.

"It seems like everything good in my life is temporary. The only constant is the ranch." His words broke her heart. She didn't want to hurt him, but she was afraid if she didn't push him away now, he was going to hurt her.

"We have another week to enjoy each other's company, and then I'm getting on the plane to Chicago and going back to reality."

"I know that, and I give you my word I'll respect your choice, but I can't shut off my feelings for you anymore than I can pack my bags and follow you to Chicago while you build your career. It almost feels like fate is playing a cruel joke on me by bringing you here to tempt me and then stealing you away. I can only hope that you will allow me to be in your life from a distance. As friends, or occasional lovers, I'll take whatever you're willing to give."

Lacy swallowed hard, and tears started sliding down her cheeks to land on the pillow under her head. "I'm not sorry. I'm not sorry that I came here, or that I met you. I care more for you than I have anyone in my life, but I can't stay. That job is the stepping stone that I need to build a legitimate business of my own, I have to take it if they offer it to me."

"Hush now..." Drannon reached out to pull her teary face against his bare chest. He pressed a kiss on the crown of her head, and she could feel him running his fingers through her hair. When was the last time someone had soothed her with such a sweet and honest touch? She couldn't remember. "Don't worry sweetheart, I know the facts, and I'm not angry with you. If you don't get the job though...well...I suppose I better just leave it. We'll cross that bridge when we come to it. Let's eat and then tuck you back into bed for some well-deserved rest. It's your birthday, and I intend on loving you as often as I can before you leave."

Chapter 10

Hours later, Lacy was absolutely sure that her body was going to need traction when she hopped the plane back to Chicago. She ached in places she hadn't ever ached before, but every twinge reminded her of the exquisite way Drannon had loved her body. She understood the phrase "making love" now because the man did nothing without emotion. It was as though they communicated more clearly without words.

After showering and dressing in the comfiest clothes she'd brought along, she headed downstairs. Drannon had headed down an hour before assuring her that he wouldn't be gone long, but she respected that he had obligations to the ranch. She wanted to check in on Marilyn to see if she was feeling better, and besides, today was the big day. The golden key to her future could be sitting in her inbox right now. The question was, did she really want to open it yet?

The sound of voices drew her through the living room to the kitchen where she found the countertops scattered with various utensils and used mixing bowls, and three men dotted with flour and what looked to be chocolate frosting.

"Lacy!" Hawke gasped, and moved to stand in front of something blocking her view. "What are you doing down here?"

"Hey guys. What are you doing?" she asked, frowning at the guilty expressions on Vin and Hawke's faces. Roman gave her a shit eating grin that indicated her gut was right and these three were up to something.

"We're taking care of the cooking while Marilyn is resting. Why aren't you resting?" Roman said, moving in her direction. He linked one arm around her waist and spun her toward the doorway. "By the smile on big D's face I wasn't expecting to see you down here until mid-week."

She felt her cheeks heat as she realized her secret fling wasn't so secret anymore. Unable to formulate a good response, she dropped her gaze to the floor and shifted nervously. To her surprise, Vin stepped closer and took her hand in his, "Hey, what's this? Are you embarrassed? You shouldn't be. We're all three happy to see D find someone who makes him happy."

While she appreciated the endorsement, she wasn't ready to have a discussion with Drannon's family about her intentions, so she changed the subject. "Thanks. I think I've spent enough time in bed. I wanted to check in on Marilyn and see if there was anything I could do to help."

"Oh, that's sweet, but she's fine. She woke up with a bit of a headache and we insisted she go back to bed. Has anyone told you how beautiful you are when you're blushing?"

Roman's flirtatious teasing made her blush harder and she was just about to give him a piece of her mind when Vin growled at him.

"Leave her alone Romeo, she's off limits." Vin's cheek had a telltale white flour mark just beneath his eye. "Drannon's out with Dorothy, but he'll be back in shortly. Did you need anything? We'd be happy to help."

"No, I'm fine. I just wanted to check in on Marilyn. What are you guys making in there?"

"Happy Valentine's Day to you, too." Hawke responded moving closer to stand beside Vin.

She rolled her eyes, and laughed. "Happy Valentine's Day."

"Sounds like you and Drannon found the spirit of love last night." Hawke teased, receiving and elbow to the ribs from Vin.

"Shut up, asshat." The bigger man snarled at his younger brother and then gave Lacy another apologetic smile. "These two heathens don't get out much. You'll have to forgive them for being jackasses. I think it's all the video games."

Roman snorted and punched Vin in the shoulder, "We're not the ones who act like hermits. When's the last time you got laid, soldier boy?"

The glare Vin gave Roman was lethal, and Lacy hurried to intercede. "No offense taken. It's nice to have such good-looking gentlemen appreciating me." Roman's face broke into a smug smile, and Hawke looked at her almost like an adoring fan. "However, Vin's right, I'm off limits. I don't know you guys very well yet, but I do know that Drannon will flip if he hears you flirting with me, and besides, I'm going back to Chicago next week."

"Just making sure you know you have options…" Roman said with a wink.

"No she doesn't." Drannon's voice echoed through the room even though he spoke quietly, and Lacy turned in his direction, sure she was going to find him livid over his brother's flirting. She found him watching her with a slight smile curving his lips.

"I always have options," she said with an irritated huff.

Drannon shook his head and came to her side, wrapping his arms around her. It was the first real display of affection in front of his family, and she wasn't sure if she should pull away or just accept it. He didn't give her a chance to decide before he kissed her. It was a soul-stealing, deeply passionate kiss that left no doubt in her mind how he felt about his brothers flirting. He might not be in an outright pissing match, but he'd more or less just marked his territory.

When he pulled away, she was gasping for air and slightly woozy. His chocolate brown eyes were dark with desire and he turned them on Roman. "Let me rephrase that. She's made her choice, and you're going to back off."

"Heard you loud and clear. Hell, I thought you were going to eat her alive right here in front of us." Roman teased.

"Shut up, Romeo." Drannon said softly, staring down at Lacy. "Did you get enough rest?"

"Yes, I slept like the dead." She was keenly aware of Vin and Hawke still silently watching their interaction, but no one seemed bothered in the least by their affectionate display. "I was just about to check on Marilyn, but these guys forced me out of the kitchen."

Drannon narrowed his eyes on Roman who shrugged and said simply, "We've got it under control. You lovebirds can roost until dinner."

Vin smacked his brother in the head making Lacy giggle as Drannon rolled his eyes.

"I was just thinking we could watch a movie on the big screen while the guys were giving the games a rest." Drannon said, pulling her in the direction of the family room. "We have hundreds of movies to pick from. What do you like?"

"Anything. I'm not much of a movie buff, but I enjoy most genres," she answered, following his lead.

"What's your favorite movie?" He pulled open one of the floor-to-ceiling cabinets along the back of the wall. Inside were hundreds of colorful plastic cases, and she felt her mouth drop open. He caught her look of surprise, and smiled, "There's not much to do around here in the winter, so we spend a lot of time watching movies."

"I guess so. Um, my favorite movie is *Forrest Gump*," she said, running her fingertip over the smooth plastic boxes in front of her as she scanned titles.

"Really? That's a bit melodramatic for my taste." He frowned, and then reached for one on the top shelf. "What about action?"

"*Terminator*? Really? You do realize I'm a chick, right?"

He laughed. "Chicks dig Schwarzenegger, don't they?"

"Not all of us. How about this one?" She pulled free a more recent crime drama and he nodded his agreement, taking it from her. "Any chance you guys have any more popcorn around here somewhere?"

"I'll get it; you get comfy."

Drannon stuck the movie in and disappeared while the opening previews were running. She sat down and pulled a blanket over her lap. It was amazing how cold it was here compared to at home. The only time she didn't feel chilled to the bone was when Drannon had her naked.

Vin appeared in the doorway with a couple of cans of soda. "D told me what you were watching; do you mind if I watch too?"

Accepting the soda, she nodded, "Sure, the more the merrier."

"*Kickass*! I love this one. The lead guy reminds me a big of my old cellmate, except that he was guilty and this actor isn't." Vin laughed at his own joke, and Lacy looked at him more closely. The dark ink of a tattoo poked just above the v-neck of his t-shirt on his chest, and his scalp was perfectly shaved. The combination gave him a bad boy look that certainly didn't fit the cowboy persona she had in mind for a ranch owner.

"What did you do?" she asked bravely.

He popped the top on his can of soda and took a sip before answering. "The first time I robbed a cigarette machine."

Lacy prompted, "Excuse me?"

"The first time I was arrested, I was seventeen, and I didn't have any money, so I broke into a cigarette machine. They put me in juvy until I turned eighteen. The judge gave me the option of going into the military or going to an adult prison, so Uncle Sam and I got on good terms."

"How long were you in the military?"

"Years. Way too long. The second time I was arrested it was because I put my fist in a guy's mouth because he was…well, it doesn't matter anymore. I was excused from the military, and I spent a year in prison before I walked free. The ranch was the only place I had to go to, and Abe wasn't the kinda guy to judge." Vin said. He turned away and Lacy let the subject drop, having a new outlook on exactly what kind of ex-cons she was staying with. Drannon had said that Vin went to prison for defending a woman, and he'd just more or less admitted that. She couldn't hate a man who put his freedom on the line for someone else.

Drannon reappeared with a big bowl of popcorn just as the movie started rolling, and they settled in for a peaceful afternoon snuggling on the couch. She couldn't help thinking that it was the best birthday she'd ever had, and certainly the best Valentine's Day.

It was almost dinner time when the movie ended, and although Lacy offered to help, the guys insisted she stay out of the kitchen.

"Can I at least go check on Marilyn now?" she asked with a frustrated sigh.

Hawke and Roman exchanged a glance and Roman shook his head. "She'll be at dinner if it makes you feel any better."

"No that doesn't make me feel better. Why are you guys keeping me from her?" Lacy nearly stomped her foot in frustration.

"We're not. We're keeping you out of the kitchen." Hawke answered automatically, earning a shove from Vin.

"Damn it, now she'll want answers," Vin growled.

Lacy looked at each of the four men, her eyes narrowing on Hawke's fidgeting. He seemed like the weakest link. "Hawke, what's going on?"

The blonde man shook his head and bit his lip, but didn't answer. Roman gave her a grin, and Vin refused to meet her gaze. Drannon finally spoke up. "It's Valentine's Day. Don't ruin the surprise."

The other three men seemed to take that as their cue to leave, and Lacy was left alone with Drannon. "You've already given me a gift…"

He shrugged. "This one isn't from me."

Emotion and curiosity blended to burn in the back of her throat. Even the suggestion that these guys would want to do something for her when they barely knew her left her overcome with adoration for all of them. Her link to this family was growing, and she was becoming more and more aware of the temporary nature of her stay.

Nodding, she shoved her hands in the pockets of her sweats. "I guess I'll go check my email then."

"Lacy, wait..." He hesitated and she turned her back to him.

"Don't say things that neither of us can handle hearing, Drannon. Not now."

His arms came around her, drawing her tight to his chest, and he pressed his face into the curve of her neck. "I won't, I promise. But if I'm going to avoid it, then so are you. Promise me you won't open that email until tomorrow."

"I—"

"Please. Let today be about us, and we'll face tomorrow soon enough." His plea meant more to her than she could have ever fathomed, and she found herself nodding in agreement without meaning to. "Good, now I think I promised to keep you in bed for Valentine's day..."

She gasped as he scooped her up into his arms. "Drannon!"

"Shh. My brothers will come looking if they think they stand a chance of swaying you away from me, and you're mine."

Her arms were locked tightly around his neck as he bounded up the stairs two at a time with her in his grip. She was in awe of his physical strength, and said as much, making him laugh. He playfully flexed for her after dropping her on his bed and stripping his shirt off.

"This man candy is all yours for tonight, baby," he teased.

She sat up and tugged her t-shirt over her head, tossing it his way when his eyes widened at her lack of a bra. "You're going to have to go easy on me. I'm a little tender."

"It's a damn good thing I didn't know you weren't wearing a bra when we were sitting under that blanket watching the movie." His breathing deepened and his eyes grew dark. Lowering to his knees in front of her, he pulled her pants off and pushed her onto her back. "If you're tender, I'll have to kiss you better again."

His mouth was hot against her core, and she squealed at the first contact, feeling moisture flood her channel. Arching her back she propped her heels on his shoulders and relaxed her thighs so that she was as open as possible for him.

"Drannon, please!" she moaned.

His only response was a breath of cool air blown right across her clit. She could see and feel her legs trembling, and she gripped her own breasts, massaging them hard as he tongued her folds. He seemed to thoroughly enjoy her taste and her reactions. The louder she begged, the firmer he pressed his mouth to her.

Just when she thought she couldn't take it anymore, he pulled back, and added his thrusting fingers to her dripping wet opening. She could feel him stretching her well-fucked pussy, easing her muscles so that she could accept him without pain, and she let her head fall back. Staring up at the ceiling she shattered around his fingers, coming harder than she'd ever come before, and screaming his name.

They connected on a soul deep level as he made love to her, and when they finally slumped together on the bed they were satisfied and silent, both dealing with their own mixed emotions. Lacy wasn't ready to admit out loud that she loved him, but she heard the words echoing in her head as a single tear slid down her cheek and soaked into the blanket beneath her.

Leaving Crawley Creek was going to kill her.

Lori King

Chapter 11

"Close your eyes." Drannon instructed as he led Lacy toward the dining room doorway.

"Seriously?" she asked, closing her eyes and shaking her head. Part of him wanted to squirrel her away upstairs for the rest of her stay and refuse to let anyone else share in any of the short time they had together, but his brothers had gone above and beyond to make tonight special. He couldn't disappoint any of them.

"Seriously. They're all waiting for us."

Roman's voice called out, "Yes we are! And we could've already eaten if you two hadn't been napping, so get in here before it gets cold."

Lacy giggled and Drannon rolled his eyes at his brothers teasing. Leading her into the dining room, he carefully blocked her view until he was sure they were ready for her. Once Vin lit the final candle, Marilyn began to sing softly.

"Happy birthday to you…happy birthday to you…"

The rest of them joined in as Lacy's eyes shot open in surprise and then automatically filled with tears. It was a strange feeling to see her crying happy tears because he wasn't sure he liked seeing her cry at all, yet she'd done it several times in the last couple of days. He knew she'd reacted to their lovemaking earlier, and it was a tough decision not to speak up and ask her about it, but he'd promised her space. He couldn't break that promise now.

"Oh, my God!" Lacy said, her trembling hands covering her lips. "You guys didn't have to do this."

In the center of the table was a casserole dish they usually used to make lasagna in, and it was filled with a lumpy looking cake covered in chocolate frosting. Several melting candles dotted the surface. His brothers all glowed with pride as Lacy reacted to their surprise.

"Sera once told me that everyone deserves a celebration of their life once a year. It's a blessing to be given one more day with family and friends, much less one more year." Hawke said, drawing everyone's attention at his surprisingly philosophical thoughts.

Lacy nodded, "She was absolutely right. Thank you. From the bottom of my heart."

"Don't thank us yet." Roman said, snorting out a laugh, "You haven't tasted it."

Marilyn shook her head, "Usually, I would have made the birthday cake, but with me not feeling so spritely today the boys got it into their heads to raid my cupboards. It's a good thing I keep a spare cake mix on hand, or who knows what you might have gotten. They threw out two different bowls of batter."

"Three." Hawke corrected, "That last one was Romeo's fault."

"How was I supposed to know there was more than one kind of sugar." Roman protested.

Drannon laughed along with the rest of his family, as Vin retrieved the dish full of pasta and sauce for their supper, and Hawke cut the cake into large slices for everyone. He watched Lacy interact with his brothers and the other woman who played such a large role in his life, and he couldn't help but fall completely over the cliff. There was no way he could lie to himself or Lacy and say this was all meaningless.

~ ~ ~ ~

"So, Marilyn, how did you come to be at Crawley Creek?" Lacy asked, redirecting the conversation as she licked frosting from her fork and then twisted spaghetti onto its tines.

The older woman took a piece of garlic bread and then replied, "I was another stray the Crawleys took in, believe it or not." She paused to take a bite and continued, "I was married to my childhood sweetheart, but he was shipped off to Vietnam four days after our wedding. He came back with a traumatic brain injury, and he was never the same. A few years after he came back, he—" She stopped, emotion clogging her voice.

Lacy was horrified, "You don't have to tell me. I'm sorry!"

Marilyn shook her head, "You would think after forty years it wouldn't hurt so much to talk about, but it does. My David committed suicide, and because he was my whole life I found myself without a purpose. Like a ship on a cloudless night with no compass. I didn't know what to do with myself. We'd had no children, and my parents were aging quickly. I met Sera at a church meeting, and we became friends. She was such a good listener… Anyways, when the money from David's life insurance ran out, I came to work for Abe and Sera, and I've never looked back. They were my guardian angels as much as they were there for these boys."

There was a heavy silence as everyone absorbed the impact of Abe and Sera Crawley's legacy. They'd been two people with large hearts that were open to everyone, and they'd managed to create a family where there was none.

"I wish I could have met them." Lacy said softly. "They sound like great people."

Drannon nodded. "The best."

"You know Sera used to wear her hair braided just like you do." Marilyn said conversationally. Lacy looked at Drannon, surprised that he hadn't mentioned that when they talked about her hair earlier.

"Really?"

"Oh, yeah," Hawke said, nodding, "I can't remember many times when her hair wasn't braided. She even used to loop it up over her head like a rope or something. I always wondered how she kept it up there."

Lacy laughed, "Women have special little devices called bobby pins and barrettes."

Hawke flushed a bit, and grinned back, "I know what a bobby pin is. I remember trying to pick the lock on Lauren's diary with one once or twice."

"Who's Lauren?" Lacy asked.

"She was one of the kids who stuck around longer than most. We took her under our wing when she came to the ranch because she was like one of the guys. She could shoot better than any man I know." Drannon said, and Lacy tasted the bitter grains of jealousy on her tongue at the pride in his voice over another woman.

"So, she's your foster sister?"

"No, she was never actually a foster kid, she just had to leave her mom's house more than once to avoid getting the shit beat out of her. Every time she went back to her mom's care she ended up back at Crawley Creek a couple of months later."

Feeling guilty that she'd been jealous, Lacy shook her head. "I can't imagine what she went through. It was good she had you guys. How many kids actually lived on the ranch?"

Everyone at the table laughed, and Drannon answered, "Too many to count. Abe always joked that he should replace the front door with one of those metal turnstile the bus station has."

"Do you still see Lauren or any of the others?"

"I talked to Lauren last week via email." Hawke said.

"You did?" Vin's eyes were wide with surprise, but his tone was rough. "Why didn't you tell me you have her email address?"

"I didn't know you wanted it," Hawke said with a shrug. "She's good. Living in Little Rock right now."

"I still talk to several of them," Roman added. "And some of them come back to see the old place every now and then. Crawley Creek leaves a mark on everyone who visits."

Lacy nodded in agreement, as she finished off her dinner, "Yes, I can see how it would. It's a special place."

She could envision what the ranch might have looked like to a child who was broken and devoid of anything special in their lives. Drannon had spoken of Abe and Sera with such pride and awe that she knew they must have been special people, but hearing about all of their good deeds made her wonder at her own life. What was she really doing to make an impact on the world? Branding a bag of puppy chow? It seemed superfluous in comparison. She wanted to share in the experience of giving a child the love they needed to grow, but a baby wouldn't fit into her future plans, and besides, she wouldn't really know what to do with one.

Drannon would be a great father. The words flitted through her brain, and she immediately cursed herself for the stray thought. She was leaving North Dakota for good next week, there was no way she should be entertaining thoughts of children with anyone. She needed to stay focused on the future, and complete the plan she had in place.

Yes. That was what she needed to do, but was it really what she wanted to do?

Chapter 12

The snow hadn't piled up as much as the weatherman predicted, but the roads were impassable because of drifting, and Drannon knew that Vin's offer to handle all of the daily chores while Lacy was at the ranch was an opportunity he couldn't ignore, so for the last couple of days they'd done nothing but enjoy each other's company. She'd resisted checking her email as far as he knew, but it would happen eventually. At some point they'd have to return to reality and he wasn't looking forward to it.

Lacy was a woman unlike any he'd ever known. She was intelligent, witty, down to earth, and as sexy as any centerfold he'd ever seen. He wanted her with a strength that came from deep in his core, and the more he had of her, the more he wanted. It was almost like an addict's obsession with their drug of choice. His body responded to her slightest touch, and he wasn't sure how he was ever going to let her go. She'd captivated him from the first moment their eyes had locked, and now she'd captured his heart. He was thankful for the chance to be with her, but with every second of silence he was contemplating how he could convince her to stay.

All his life he'd lost the things that were important to him. His mother, his career, his marriage, even his freedom for a time. Why should he have to give up this happiness? He knew Lacy had a career goal, and he had no business asking her to give up her dreams, yet he couldn't help imagining a future with her staying on the ranch. They would open their doors to foster children just as Abe and Sera had, and build a life here on the family ranch as he'd envisioned himself doing.

"Hello?"

Her voice broke into his deepest thoughts, and he looked down to where she was lying cradled against his side, her head on his chest. Her brown eyes were staring at him with rapt curiosity, and her lips curled up in a sexy smile.

"There you are. What's got you so quiet all of a sudden?" she asked.

For just a moment, he considered laying his heart bare. Telling her everything, and letting her turn him down flat. Being heartbroken would be easier now, rather than in a few days when she had to leave, but he couldn't do it.

"Nothing. I thought you were drifting back to sleep, so I was trying to let you rest." He ran his fingertips over the curve of her hip. Her skin was petal soft, and she smelled slightly flowery from their shower before they'd tumbled into bed the night before.

"I don't usually fall right to sleep after sex, but I have to admit, you've worn me out lately." She teased, pinching his nipple.

"Ouch, hey!"

"It's only fair that I get to do to you what you've done to me," she said, pinching the other nipple.

He feigned shock and let out a small growl. "Women don't play with men's nipples."

"Oh really?" She sat up slightly so that she could put her mouth over the nipple closest to her, and he gasped at the tingling sensation. She looked pleased when she pulled back. "You can't tell me you don't like it."

"It's not manly," he argued. He loved her playful side.

She slid her hand to his cock which was thickening once again in spite of the exhausting efforts of the past night. "Feels pretty manly to me."

"Keep it up and he'll prove how manly he is." Drannon teased.

"I'm not sure I can go again," she said with a giggle. "My body is aching, big time."

A shaft of pride went through him that he was the man who brought her to the edge over and over leaving her exhausted and satisfied. Pulling her flush against him, he kissed her softly, putting every ounce of emotion inside of him into the connection between their lips. Even if she wasn't ready to hear him say the words, he needed to show his feelings somehow. With slow, sensuous movements, he made gentle, sweet love to her again.

~ ~ ~ ~

It took nearly a week for Lacy to gather her courage and turn on her laptop. They had yet to lose power at the ranch, but to her the twelve inches or so of snow was a blizzard of monumental proportions. Drannon just laughed it off as a small snow burst. The temperatures were bitter cold, and late in the afternoon the wind seemed to blow the snow so it was almost impossible to tell if it was snowing again, or just whipping up the same old stuff. As beautiful as the surrounding environment was, she knew she couldn't keep burying her head in the blankets and pretending everything was okay, so today when Drannon went out to check on Dorothy, she made her way downstairs to the study.

The door was open, and she found Vin draped over the dainty chaise lounge. His massive frame dwarfed the piece of furniture in a comical way and she giggled drawing his attention from the book he was reading.

"Lacy, hey." He hurried to sit up and find a more upright position as she moved into the room.

"Oh don't mind me. I just came down to get online for a bit." She said, heading across the room to take a seat at the large desk.

Vin let out a heavy sigh, and put his book on the coffee table. "Time to get back to the real world, huh?"

She nodded, and bit her lip to keep from tearing up. The last thing she wanted to do was show Drannon's brother how much leaving would affect her.

"Does D know you're still planning on leaving?" Vin asked.

"Yes, we've talked about it. I can't just drop everything and move to another state for a man I've just met."

Vin's blue eyes narrowed, and he leaned forward propping his elbows on his knees. "What's stopping you?"

She wanted to tell him that it was her career, and her dreams for the future, but she heard herself answering, "Fear."

He nodded as though that was the answer he'd expected. "Yeah, I can see that. You know, when I got out of prison I was terrified that I wouldn't be welcome on the ranch, but Abe was sitting outside the gate in his beat up pick-up truck the day I was released ready to take me back. He never asked me why I'd done what I'd done, he just accepted that I'd paid the price for my actions and wiped the slate clean."

"Can I ask what happened?" she said warily.

"Drannon and I were at a bar while I was home for a couple of weeks, and there was this guy there with his girlfriend and his buddies. He was acting like a drunk douchebag, saying shitty things about military men, and me and D in general, but I was holding my temper in check. We were getting ready to leave and I had to take a piss—er—sorry—I had to use the facilities. That same jackass had his girl pinned to the wall in the hallway and he was hurting her. I couldn't walk away and leave her, so I broke a bottle over his head to get his attention, and then broke his nose."

"Ouch. So how did you end up in jail if you were trying to help her?"

"That's the kicker of the whole night. His girl told the police that she was just fine and they were just having a lover's quarrel that I got in the middle of. Her words sealed my fate when the scumbag decided to press charges for assault."

"Wow." Lacy whispered, wondering at a system that would put a man in jail for defending a woman.

"Yeah, it was a low point in my life that's for sure. Uncle Sam cut me loose when I pled guilty to the charges, and I had to do my time. I wish to hell it'd played out different, but it is what it is." Vin shrugged his big shoulders, and rose to his feet. "I guess my point is that you can't always determine the outcome of something before it happens. Maybe it turns out great, but maybe it goes to hell and you get hurt. You'll never know if you never take the risk. I know my brother. He's been my salvation and my rock since I was seven years old, and I have to tell you, if you walk away it will break him."

"Vin—" Lacy started to protest his involvement. He didn't know all of the facts.

"No, listen. He's in love with you, Lacy, and whether you've said it out loud or not I know you feel the same about him. Don't give up a chance at something good because it wasn't on your prewritten plan to happiness. Plans change, sometimes for the best." With that Vin picked up his book and headed to the door.

"Vin," she called out, and he turned around. "Thanks. You're a good brother to him."

The muscular man nodded, and gave her a smile, "Yeah, I am, but only because he taught me how to be." Turning away he disappeared out the door leaving Lacy to face a monumental decision alone.

It took her another half an hour to open her inbox. She goofed around wasting as much time as she could, and avoiding the inevitable. When she clicked open the file, her worst fears and greatest joys were in front of her. The email was there. She got the job. If she wanted it, she needed to be back in Chicago by March first.

Based on her original reservations with the ranch and her flight plans that would work just fine, but instead of feeling excitement, Lacy's stomach was in a ball of dread.

Accepting the job meant leaving Drannon and Crawley Creek behind. In just days, everything she thought she knew about her life had changed. She was no longer Lacy Denvers, career-driven, motherless loner who avoided entanglements.

Now she was Drannon's sweetheart, and an entrepreneur who could telecommute if she wanted. As long as she didn't take the dog food company's account she could work from anywhere in the world. If she took it, she would have the substance on her resume to build a solid company, and if she didn't take it, she could face months if not years of mediocre jobs that would barely pay her regular bills much less push her career forward. It was a virtual Catch-22, because taking it would mean giving up what she had with Drannon for good.

After mulling over the job offer for twenty minutes or so, she shut her laptop without responding to it. It physically hurt to think about packing her bags and walking off the ranch next week, but the fear of staying sat like a lump in her throat, choking out her logical thoughts.

As she thought about all of the things that had occurred in the last four days, the biggest one was the simplicity of Drannon's gift to her for her birthday and Valentine's Day. Instead of trying to buy her a gift that was expensive and lavish, he'd given her a piece of his heart. He showed her something that was special to him, and in doing so, he'd reached deep inside her soul and soothed a part of her that had been aching all of her life. Her father hadn't even been able to do that.

Her father.

It was in that moment Lacy realized her father hadn't even bothered to call her on her birthday. Perhaps he was busy with work, or just forgot, but it still hurt. Thirty years had passed since Lacy was born and her mother died, yet the man still hadn't been able to forgive the child he blamed for his wife's death.

He had spent her whole life holding his affection back from his daughter out of anger and hurt, hiding away from the world in order to keep from getting hurt again. In fact, now that she thought about it, his example was where she learned to hide herself away behind a computer. She had always preferred indirect interaction with her peers because they couldn't hurt her if she kept the distance between them. Was she doing that now with Drannon?

Was she using the job offer as an excuse to avoid taking a risk and possibly getting hurt? It was all so clear...or was it?

Lacy surged to her feet from behind the desk and ran to the bedroom. She was a woman on a mission now, and nothing would stop her.

~ ~ ~ ~

"Lacy?"

Her father's voice sounded confused, and she hurried to respond.

"Hi Dad. How are you?"

"Good. How are you?"

She felt her stomach twist in a knot. They sounded like acquaintances, not like a father and daughter.

"I'm great. In fact, I have some news."

"Oh? What's that?"

"I got fired."

He was silent for several moments before he asked, "And that's good news?"

"Yes, it is." She giggled into her cell phone imagining the look on Leo Denvers' face. "Because I got fired, I decided to start my own company and take a vacation."

"Well that's good. Where did you go?"

"North Dakota. I'm there now, in fact."

"That's not the first place I would have guessed, but I hope you're enjoying your stay."

"I am, but that's not all. See, I wanted to come here because I've always wanted to ride a horse, and you never let me as a kid."

"What? It's not like we had a stable full—"

"Wait, I didn't mean that the way it sounded. I just meant that I wanted to fulfill a childhood dream, and in doing so, I actually met someone. Drannon Russo."

"And this Drannon is important to you now?"

"He is. In fact, I think he's more important to me than my career is."

Leo was silent on the other end of the phone, but Lacy let the silence hold. She wasn't going to do her father's job anymore. If he had something to say, he needed to say it.

"I'm happy for you, but dear, you know that vacation romances don't usually last."

"I know, but I also know that's not what this is. Can I ask you something, Dad, and you have to promise to answer me honestly?"

"Of course, Lacy, what is it?"

"If you'd known about mom's health problem, would you have asked her to give up the pregnancy?"

Dead silence filled the phone line between them again, and she nervously picked at her nails while she waited for the answer she didn't want to hear. When her father spoke again his voice was tight with emotion.

"I don't know. I loved your mom Lacy. She was my entire world."

"I know, but Dad she loved me that much. So much that she was willing to give up everything to give me life."

"She should have told me."

"Yep, she should have, but would it have changed anything?"

Leo sighed heavily. "No probably not. Your mother was stubborn, and she had a plan for her life. She wanted a family, and nothing was going to stop her from having one."

"I know someone like that," Lacy said with a small laugh.

"I didn't know how to be a dad, Lacy, but I did try my best."

"I'm in love with Drannon, Dad, and although he hasn't said it yet, I know he loves me, too. I'm staying in North Dakota, Dad. I just wanted you to know because you're my father."

"Okay. I hope you're not doing this because you lost your job."

"No, that might be the reason I ended up on the ranch, but it's not the reason I'm staying. I've just recently realized that the best laid plans should always be written in pencil because they're going to change."

"Your mother would be proud of you, Lacy." Tears clogged Lacy's throat, and she sniffed into the phone without responding.

"Well, best of luck to you both. I need to go. I have a dinner engagement tonight."

"Okay. I'll talk to you later then."

"Oh, and Lacy? Happy birthday."

She choked on her pain, and in that moment, she realized that her father was who he was, and it wasn't up to her to change him. It was more important that she change her expectations, and live her life based on her own needs. He was right, her mother would have encouraged her to pursue love, and she would have been proud of her.

"Thanks Dad. Have a good night."

The click of the phone was his only response, and Lacy brushed her tears away. With a new iron-clad understanding of what she needed in this life, she tossed her phone on her bed, and went to send an email to the dog food company. Once she clicked *Send*, she could get on with her life.

~ ~ ~ ~

Drannon was in the barn again when she found him in the middle aisle doing something with the stirrup on a saddle. He looked up and smiled. "Hey! You should be inside where it's warm. What are you doing out here, sweetheart?"

"I was just inside checking my email, and there was a response from the company I've been waiting to hear from."

His smile was still on his face, but his eyes dimmed. "Really? What did they say?"

She moved close, holding her surprise tightly behind her back so that he wouldn't see it. "They offered me the job. I can start March first."

His shoulders visibly deflated, but he continued to smile with forced joy on his face. "That's great. They'll be lucky to have you."

"There's only one problem..." She paused, and his smile slipped from his face. "You see, something special happened on Valentine's Day this year, and I've suddenly found that I can't take that job."

Hope flashed in his brown eyes as she drew close enough to reach out to him. Pressing one hand to his chest, she leaned forward, and he had to tip his head to hold her gaze. "Do you see this..."—she gestured and he took her arm in his big hands, making her wrist look tiny against them—"here on my wrist?"

"That's a rope burn. Damn, I'm sorry sweetheart..."

"That's right; it's a rope burn, because a big, sexy cowboy roped me for Valentine's Day this year. He tied me down and had his wicked way with me."

Drannon's eyes slid from tawny to green and his nostrils flared. "And what's a little scrap like you going to do about it?"

"Nothing. I'm happy to be tied down for him. In fact,"—she held up the rope she was hiding behind her back and grinned wickedly—"I'm hoping he'll let me have a go at roping him this time."

Drannon's adam's apple bobbed as he swallowed, and Lacy felt his cock thicken against her stomach. "What are you saying, sweetheart?"

"I'm saying that I want to stay. For now, for a while, forever if you'll have me. I came to North Dakota a sad and lonely shell of a woman who had no idea what it was like to take a risk and enjoy a little freedom. Somehow, I've found myself falling in love with a cowboy who had a soul-deep wound of his own, and needed me. If you still want me—"

"I want you!" He interrupted her with a hard kiss on her lips. "I love you, Lacy Denvers, and I want you, for now, for a while, and forever. Roped and tied to my bed, or riding Toto through the hills. I love you."

"Good, because, cowboy, it's your turn for a little rope burn," she answered with a wicked smile as she rose up on her toes and kissed him with every ounce of love she never knew she had.

Who knew that this year she would find the best Valentine's birthday gift ever...

A cowboy.

Epilogue

Lacy woke to a cool breeze against her warm skin, and she blinked in the moonlit room.

"Wake up, Sleeping Beauty."

She turned to find Drannon lying next to her, the covers having been pulled off her and bunched between them. A wave of *déjà vu* washed over her, and she frowned at him.

"Haven't we done this before?"

His laughter wiped away any irritation she might have had at being woken in the middle of the night, and she scooted closer to him, pressing her body as close to him as she could.

He kissed her forehead. "I've got something special to show you."

"I've seen it. Last night, I saw it twice before I fell asleep. If we keep going at this rate, your pecker will fall off from overuse." She grumbled, nuzzling his collarbone.

"Not that, you perv." He rolled off the bed, and stood looking down at her naked form. "Damn. If you keep looking at me like that I might change my mind about the whole thing." He tweaked her nipple and she giggled.

"What time is it?"

He shrugged. "Early, or late depending on how you look at it. Come on. Out of bed, sleepy head."

He passed her her clothes and waited by the window as she dressed. Her curiosity piqued, she followed along silently as they moved through the quiet house and out the front door. She was thankful there was no need for cold weather gear in the middle of June, but she found herself shivering with anticipation instead.

Drannon noticed and instantly grew concerned. "Do you want me to go back and grab your jacket?"

"No, I'm good. I'm still waking up, but I'll be fine. What are we going to see?"

Unlike last time, Toto was nowhere to be seen, and Drannon was leading her into the pitch black yard. The one thing she'd yet to get used to living here was the vastness of the space around them. In the daylight, she could see for miles in almost every direction, and at night that same expansive feeling turned claustrophobic.

"Shhh, we don't want to disturb them if we can help it." Drannon tugged open the heavy barn door and directed her into the stuffy space. The smell of animals and hay filled her nostrils, and she smiled. Who'd have thought that it would all become so familiar to her after only a few months?

A soft sound drew her attention to Dorothy's stall, and she knew what he'd brought her to see. "Oh, my God!" She tried to keep her voice down. "The foal! She had her baby?" Rushing to the wooden plank enclosure, she stood in awe as she took in mama and baby.

The tiny foal was its mother's mini-me, and looked beautifully awkward moving on spindly legs around the small space.

"Aww, I've never seen anything so cute in my life. How's mama?" she asked Drannon as he moved up to stand behind her, his hands resting on her hips.

"Mama's great, and so is baby. It's a girl, and she's perfectly healthy."

Dorothy whinnied a bit, and Lacy laughed. "Of course she is. She's one of Dorothy's babies. Isn't that right, sugar?"

The horse lifted her nose closer to the gate, accepting Lacy's affectionate pat to her nose. She and Dorothy had become fast friends even though Toto was still Lacy's regular mount. The whole ranch had been anxiously awaiting the overdue birth of this baby.

"When did—"

"Hawke came and got me a few hours ago. She was nearly done by the time we got here. Just like a woman to do things on her own time," Drannon said playfully, kissing Lacy gently.

"You like it when I do things my way, so I don't want to hear it. Thank you for waking me. I'm so glad I got to see her."

Drannon shook his head, and tugged her away from Dorothy's stall, "That's not all of the surprise. Come on, Hawke should have everything ready."

Following along in confusion, Lacy was flabbergasted to find Toto saddled and ready just outside the barn. How had Hawke managed to do that?

"All set for you, D. I'm gonna go in and catch some Zs while I still can." Hawke said, passing the reins to Drannon.

"Thanks, Hawke. I owe you."

The blonde man kissed Lacy's cheek and whispered, "Have fun," before he disappeared into the darkness in the direction of the house. Her eyes had adjusted to the moonlight now, and she could see that Toto was saddled, and a blanket was draped over his neck.

"What's the blanket for?" she asked as Drannon gracefully lifted himself into the saddle and reached for her. She was seated in front of him in the blink of an eye, and she settled back comfortably against his chest.

"You'll see. Be patient."

That was all Drannon would say. She tried several times to get him to tell her where he was taking her, and when she realized they were headed in the direction of the Turtle Mountains, she tried to get him to confirm their destination.

"We're going the same way as last time. Are you taking me to the valley for an early-morning camping trip? If so, I should have grabbed a few supplies before we left." Her voice was the only recognizable sound. Creatures in the trees called out to their relations, and the dense growth on the forest floor crackled beneath Toto's hooves.

She was out of her mind with frustration and curiosity when the break in the trees appeared, and she got her first glimpse of the mountain range. The peaks were lit up by the just-risen sun, but the valley was still in heavy shadow.

"That's pretty," she marveled. "I bet the sunrise is phenomenal from up on the mountain."

Drannon nodded as he climbed down off of Toto. He helped her down and rubbed the small of her back when she stretched her muscles. "Come on, we don't have much time."

She followed along as he took the blanket and Toto's reins and led her to a rock ledge that seemed to hover over the valley floor unsupported. It was a half circle about eight feet wide at its widest point.

"You want me to go on there? Is it safe?" she asked warily.

Drannon rolled his eyes. "Sweetheart, I wouldn't risk your safety. It's a piece of a much larger boulder, and it's been here for centuries, I'm sure. We can stay back here, but you'll get the best view from the ledge."

Swallowing back her fear, Lacy took his hand and carefully moved onto the platform. Drannon spread the blanket on the rock, and then gestured for her to sit down.

"What are we doing here?" she asked.

"Watch. It should happen in the next few minutes." He propped his back against the cliff, and she leaned into him, grateful for his support even if they were on stable ground. Turning her eyes in the direction of the mountains again, she watched for something spectacular.

It was a couple of minutes before she realized that the line of light was traveling slowly down the mountain as the sun crept higher in the sky. With every foot gained, more of the breathtaking vista came into view, and she heard herself gasp with delight as a blue carpet of flowers spread out in front of them.

"The forget-me-nots!" she exclaimed, remembering his comments months ago about this being his favorite place and time. He'd brought her to share it with him, and that meant the world to her. Each day, he seemed to show her more how much he loved her, but this was overwhelming. Tears slid down her cheeks as she stared out at the majestic site before her. It was the perfect combination of strong mountains and soft flowers. No artist could have done it justice. "It's magnificent. So beautiful."

"I knew you'd like it." Drannon shifted, turning to face her, and pulling her hands into his. "Lacy Denvers, I realize we've only known each other for a few months, and before I met you I laughed at the notion that someone could fall in love so quickly, but that's exactly what happened. I love you more than anything else in the world, and I want to watch the sunrise with you every day for the rest of my life." Dropping to his knee, he slid a small white velvet box from his pocket. "Will you marry me?"

Lacy swallowed hard, struggling to keep control of her emotions. As always humor was her first reaction, "I'm not much of a morning person, but if you'll consider sunsets rather than sunrises…"

Drannon laughed, and shook his head. "As long as you say yes."

"Yes! Of course yes! I love you Drannon Russo, and I'll never forget this moment for as long as I live." Their kiss broke any record they'd already set for passion, as they both poured their hearts into the connection.

When they separated, he held up the box and laughed, "Are you going to look at the ring?"

"Yes!" she snatched the box and clicked it open to find a ruby and diamond engagement ring inside. Eyes wet with tears, and cheeks hurting because her smile was so wide, she slid it on her finger. "It's beautiful."

"I picked it out while you were packing up your stuff in Chicago last March, but I wanted to give you some time before I asked. The color reminded me of your hair when it's wet." He said, kissing the spot on her finger where the ring rested.

"You're perfect for me, cowboy. I would have said yes then, too, but I'm glad you waited. I will enjoy telling this story to our grandkids someday." She whispered, wrapping her arms around the man of her dreams.

As her future husband began to make love to her, Lacy couldn't help but think how lucky she was, and how glad she was that she'd taken a leap of faith. With Hawke's ingenuity, and her skills in marketing, the ranch was already well on its way to becoming a therapeutic retreat for individuals seeking solace from their demons. Soon they would have their first foster child on the ranch, and a new therapist was scheduled to start a permanent position at Crawley Creek next month.

Her future was clear, and as bright as the sunshine kissing the valley below them.

The End

EXCERPT:

Rough Ride Romeo
(Crawley Creek 2)

Chapter 1

The sound of an engine shattered Roman Freemont's peaceful snoring, and he choked on an inhale fumbling awake. His mouth tasted like shit, and his tongue felt like it had been sanded down with fine grit sandpaper. The haze in his vision could have been his hangover, or a thick fog bank, but considering the height of the sunshine beating down through the windshield, he was more apt to assume the former.

Shoving a hand through his shoulder length brown hair, he encountered something sticky matting the ends of several pieces, and grimaced. It wasn't like this was the first time he'd slept off an all-nighter in his truck, but this wasn't even the first time this week. He could already feel Drannon and Vin's disapproval, and he hadn't even seen them yet this morning. Hell, the sensation was strong enough that the hair on his neck prickled.

Rubbing at his nape with one hand, he searched the scattered contents of his old Chevy pickup for his cell phone. As usual, its battery was completely dead, but he figured there were a dozen messages from the ranch already filling his inbox. He tossed the useless gadget into the glove compartment, and climbed out of the truck, stretching his long, lean form as he went. Drinking and cavorting were the only medicine for the aches in his soul, but he could use some aspirin for the twinges in his back right about now.

A quick glance around the parking lot of Mick's Watering Hole assured him that there was no one watching his walk of shame. There were half a dozen vehicles on the far side of the lot, but they all stood empty, their owners off doing their business somewhere along the six block town of Montford, North Dakota.

With no one watching, he made his way across the empty lot to the convenience store next door. His head was pounding, and he could still taste the bitters from last night's beer. The small bell attached to the glass door sounded like an air raid siren, and he groaned softly.

"Morning Romeo." Amelia Dewitt called out from her stool behind the register.

"Roman Freemont, you look like shit." Brandon Bowers rested his hip against the countertop and crossed his arms over his chest. His eyes were hidden behind a pair of mirrored sunglasses, but Roman knew they were taking in his hangover and cataloguing it in detail. Lately it was Roman's natural state.

"Well good morning to you, too, sunshine," he retorted, heading straight for the cold case at the back and snagging a large bottle of pop. Caffeine would help him face the day while it was too early to drink.

Bran didn't respond to his comment, but Roman could tell he had something he wanted to say just by the way his jaw ticked. Ignoring his friend for the moment, he placed a bottle of aspirin on the counter next to his soda and gave Amelia his most charming smile. "And how are you this fine morning Amelia?"

"Better than you are I s'pose," she answered with a playful wink. Her graying hair was wound in a tight bun atop her head, and her plastic framed glasses perched on the end of her nose. She was a comforting staple in small town Montford, and one of the nicest people Roman knew.

"I'll admit I'm feeling a bit low this morning, but it's nothing a hard day of work won't cure." Roman responded.

"Day's half gone already, son. You'd better get a move on if you're planning on accomplishing anything before the sun goes down." Handing him his change, she planted herself back on her stool and rested her elbows on the counter. Before Roman could respond, Bran laughed.

"No worries there, Amelia. Romeo here wouldn't know hard work if it bit him in the ass." Still laughing at his own joke, Bran slapped Roman on the back hard enough to bring a frown to his face.

"Kiss my grits, Officer," he snapped, throwing back the aspirin and taking a big swig of soda to wash it down.

"That's Sheriff Bowers to you, Freemont." Bran said sternly. To a stranger it might have sounded like the two men were at odds, but that was the absolute furthest thing from the truth. A couple of decades ago,

Brandon was one of Roman's biggest idols. He could remember following the three musketeers—also known as Roman's older foster brothers, Drannon, and Vin, who were best friends with Brandon—all over their small town and out into cattle country. Hell, they'd even taken him camping and fishing with them a time or two before they forgot about everything but girls.

Irony seemed to be waving a red flag at Roman as he stood there in the small shop. Now he was the one hell-bent on screwing his way into an early grave, and Brandon was walking the fine line of the law.

"Whatever you say, Sheriff." Roman drew out the last word pointedly. "You're right about one thing, Amelia, I need to get my ass in gear. Good to see you Bran, do be careful when you take that stick out of your ass tonight after your shift." He turned and gave Bran a hefty slap on the shoulder before marching toward the doors again.

"Don't be going too fast now, Romeo, or I won't have a chance to admire that fine backside you're planning on working," Amelia called out giving him a wave, and laughing. He blew her a kiss as he stepped back out into the blinding sunshine.

It was already hot outside, and he could feel the sweat and grime from the night before clinging to his skin as he fidgeted and stretched taking in the small main street of Montford. The town consisted of about ten thousand people nowadays, but it wasn't so long ago that it was pea-skin small and barely kept up with the couple dozen businesses that occupied the main thoroughfare. It seemed as if the whole town took a breath and then multiplied all at once. Before you knew it, they even had their own big box store down the highway a bit. He'd recently heard that a popular fast food joint would be coming to town, but until he saw the arches, he wasn't buying the story.

With a snap and a crack, his back twisted and he sighed in relief as the tension eased out of his cramped body. It was past time he went back to sleeping in a bed rather than slumped on the bench seat of his pickup, but he'd be damned if he'd drive drunk again. He was tired of the lectures every morning from the peanut gallery. Between his three brothers, Drannon, Vin, and Hawke, and Drannon's fiancé, Lacy, he had to relive his mistakes almost daily anymore. After their makeshift mama-bear Marilyn told him she was too disappointed in him to even comment on his state last time, he couldn't even bring himself to face her anymore. A quiet voice in his head reminded him that if he wasn't drunk it wouldn't be a problem, but he hushed it real quick. Life was meant to be lived, damn it. He was just enjoying it with a beer in his hand, that's all.

Taking another swig of his pop, he headed back to his truck with his beat-up straw hat pulled low over his brow to block the cheerful sun. The familiar scent of tobacco and animals filled his nose as he planted himself in the driver's seat and shoved the keys into the ignition. Throwing the gear shift in the general direction of drive, his heart nearly burst from his chest when his truck rolled backward into the parking stall behind him instead of easing forward out of the lot. The sound of grinding metal was followed by a loud crash and a woman's scream.

Also By Lori King

Crawley Creek Series
Beginnings
Forget Me Knot
Rough Ride Romeo
Claiming His Cowgirl
Sunnyside Up
Hawke's Salvation
Handcuffed by Destiny

Fetish & Fantasy
Watching Sin
Submission Dance
Mistress Hedonism
Masquerade

Surrender Series
Weekend Surrender
Flawless Surrender
Primal Surrender
Broken Surrender
Fantasy Surrender

The Gray Pack Series
Fire of the Wolf
Reflections of the Wolf
Legacy of the Wolf
Dreams of the Wolf
Caress of the Wolf
Honor of the Wolf

Apache Crossing
Sidney's Triple Shot

Sunset Point
Point of Seduction

Tempting Tanner

About the Author

Best-selling author, Lori King, is also a full-time wife and mother of three boys. Although she rarely has time to just enjoy feminine pursuits; at heart she is a hopeless romantic. She spends her days dreaming up Alpha men, and her nights telling their stories. An admitted TV and book junkie, she can be found relaxing with a steamy story, or binging in an entire season of some show online. She gives her parents all the credit for her unique sense of humor and acceptance of all forms of love. There are no two loves alike, but you can love more than one with your whole heart.

With the motto: Live, Laugh, and Love like today is your only chance, she will continue to write as long as you continue to read. Thank you for taking the time to indulge in a good Happily Ever After with her. Find out more about her current projects at http://lorikingbooks.com, or look her up on Facebook: http://www.facebook.com/LoriKingBooks or Twitter: https://twitter.com/LoriKingBooks

SIGN UP FOR LORI'S FREE NEWSLETTER!
http://lorikingbooks.com/index.php/newsletter

Made in the USA
Charleston, SC
08 January 2017